TEA IS FOR TEARS

A HAUNTED TEAROOM COZY MYSTERY

KAREN SUE WALKER

Note from the Publisher: The recipes contained in this book have been tested, and to our knowledge are correct if followed exactly as written. Cooking and baking are subject to variables outside of our control; we are not responsible for results due to errors or typos in the ingredients or instructions. The publisher and author are not responsible for any adverse reactions to the recipes contained in this book.

Note from Author: I've done my very best to make sure these recipes are accurate and will provide great results, but I must admit that I am not perfect (no matter how hard I try!)

ACKNOWLEDGMENTS

My gorgeous cover was designed by Mariah Sinclair, the Cozy Cover Queen. You can find her at https://www.thecovervault.com or on Facebook.

Thank you to Alyssa Lynn Palmer for your copyediting expertise.

Special thanks to my beta readers, typo catchers, and early reviewers—I'm so grateful to you for your support!

Finally, to my wonderful readers. Without you, I wouldn't be having nearly as much fun as I am. Keep on sending me those emails with suggestions, ideas, and pictures of your cats and dogs!

Sign up for email updates at https://karensuewalker.com and I'll do my best to keep your inbox full of everything cozy.

CHAPTER 1

*A*fter several busy days running Serenity Tearoom, Monday was my day of rest. I had planned to take a long walk along the beach to start my day, but the weather had other ideas.

Sheets of water rolled off the side of my Victorian home, filling the yard with puddles. Rainy days were made for cooking and baking, so I stayed indoors, testing new recipes. The warm kitchen filled with tantalizing aromas.

Chef Emile Toussaint, the French chef raised in Louisiana who haunted my kitchen, had promised to help me make an authentic Cajun jambalaya. Since he was a ghost, that meant he barked orders while I did all the work.

Jennifer bounced into the kitchen as I finished dicing an onion, her sandy blond hair in a high ponytail.

Oh, to be young again. It had been decades since I'd had a bounce in my step like hers.

"What's wrong?" Jennifer asked.

"Huh?" I wiped away a tear. "Oh, it's just the onions. I forgot to put them in the freezer earlier."

"Does that keep them from making you cry?" she asked. "I've heard that breathing through your mouth works. Or using a super sharp knife."

"I've also heard to hold a piece of bread in your mouth, but I would feel too silly to try it. Having a nice cold onion is the one tip that does work." I moved on to chopping the garlic, celery, and green bell peppers. I didn't care for bell peppers, but Chef Emile wouldn't hear of me leaving out such an important ingredient.

Chef leaned over my shoulder and tutted his disapproval. "That is not enough *poivron*."

I glared at him over my shoulder. I assumed he meant bell peppers, but I couldn't ask him while Jennifer was in the room.

"You will ruin the dish," Chef grumbled. "Why must I be destined to share my talents with a stubborn woman who does not recognize my superior culinary skills?" He flung his arms in the air. "Why must I be stuck here in this kitchen with such an amateur?"

My shoulders tensed as I felt my anger build. I stopped in the middle of chopping and took a few deep breaths to calm myself.

"You look angry," Jennifer said. "Are the bell peppers making you mad? Why don't you leave them out?"

"*Sacré bleu!*" Chef cried out. "I am surrounded by barbarians."

"Apparently," I said, doing my best to tune out the Chef's rant, "they're an important ingredient."

"If you say so," she said.

One of these days I'd have to tell Jennifer about the chef, but I worried about how she'd react. Would she think I was crazy? Would she quit her job?

"I'm meeting a friend in Somerton for some shopping later. Do you need me to pick up anything while I'm there?"

Before I could answer, a knock on the back door caught our attention, and our neighbor and friend Irma Vargas appeared. A cranky senior with a heart of gold who stood barely five feet tall, she owned the Mermaid Cafe, the only fine dining restaurant in town. Unlike Jennifer, she knew all about my chef-ghost.

Irma waved her umbrella toward the back door, flinging water on the floor. "What's going on out there? There's some old guy out in the pouring rain moving rocks around. I hope your insurance is up to date in case he drops dead from heart failure. Or drowns in this monsoon."

I did my best not to roll my eyes. "George Zabrowski came very well recommended. And he's got a younger guy helping him, though I've only seen him through the window." I left out the part about how handsome his helper was. "George is building me a secret garden."

Irma scowled. "How do you expect to keep it a secret?"

I laughed. "A secret garden like in the book. He's going to build a wall with a wooden gate, and inside there will be lots of beautiful plants and flowers. The old elm tree will be a focal point, and George has promised to be careful not to harm it."

"We'll have a swing, too," Jennifer said, giving me her sweetest smile. "I hope. That's my one request."

"We can use it for special events," I explained. "Or when I need to escape from the hectic life of a tearoom owner."

Irma took a seat at the island. "I'll have to see it before I decide what I think about it. What are you cooking?"

"Jambalaya." I added the onions to the hot skillet, along with garlic and the rest of the vegetables, and listened to them sizzle. "Chef Emile doesn't think there are enough bell peppers." I caught myself and said, "What I mean to say is that his recipe calls for more peppers." I glanced at Jennifer who'd busied herself cleaning the espresso machine.

Irma gave me a wink. "He's right. It's an important ingredient."

"Fine," I grumbled and began cutting up more peppers.

Chef Emile put his hands on his hips and jutted his chin in the air. "You listen to her and not me? I have better things to do than waste my time and talents on you." He faded away to nothing, but I knew he'd be back.

"I came by to let you know tonight's soup is lobster bisque," Irma said, "but I suppose you've already got your dinner figured out. I got a good deal on lobster—it's usually too expensive for my budget." She gave me a quizzical look. "I don't see a teapot. Are you telling me you don't have a pot of tea brewing?"

"I don't live only on tea, you know. Sometimes I drink water or even juice. I've been too busy cooking to make a pot."

Jennifer hurried over to the counter and grabbed the electric kettle. "I'll start a pot before I go." She filled up the kettle with filtered water, then retrieved the teapot from the cupboard and filled it with my favorite loose tea—a mix of Darjeeling and rose petals. As soon as the water boiled, she filled the pot and left it to steep for a few minutes.

"Have fun with your friend," I said as Jennifer gathered up her things and gave me a hug before leaving me alone with Irma.

Irma picked up her phone and scowled at the screen. "You know about the recall campaign against Sheriff Fontana, don't you?"

I stopped in the middle of setting out teacups and saucers and turned to her. "Why would anyone want to recall the sheriff? He's done a great job since he got the position, and he seems really popular."

"Turns out someone decided they want to get rid of him."

"Who?" I asked, figuring it must be some outsider with an agenda.

"No one seems to know, but my vote would be Chief Deputy Sheriff, Arthur Rugger. As second in command, he'd take over as sheriff if the recall was successful."

"Really?" I poured us each a cup of tea and took a

sip of mine, inhaling the floral scent. "If that's true, that would be really awkward."

"Especially because Fontana and Rugger used to be best friends." Irma plucked a sugar cube from the bowl and dropped it into her teacup. "I'm guessing that's why Rugger's keeping it a secret. But Rugger doesn't have deep pockets, so someone else must be bankrolling the effort."

When Irma finished her tea, along with a couple of shortbread cookies I'd baked earlier, she stood and grabbed her umbrella. "I guess I'll see you tomorrow."

"Oh, no," I said with a grin. "You'll see me tonight. I'm not missing out on lobster bisque. The jambalaya will be just as good tomorrow—maybe even better."

Dinnertime approached, but Jennifer hadn't returned from her visit to Somerton. I sent her a text message suggesting she join me later at the Mermaid Cafe. She must have been having a good time with her friend because she didn't respond.

As I stepped out onto the front porch, a heavy drizzle greeted me. I pulled the hood up on my jacket and crossed the street, talking myself out of going back for my car. The weather report forecast a clear night, and I looked forward to a star-filled sky on my walk home.

Soon, I was sitting at the bar with a big bowl of creamy lobster bisque along with thick slices of warm, crusty French bread. As I blew on the first spoonful of soup, a young woman stepped up next to me. Her eyes searched the room.

With purple pigtails and torn jeans, she reminded me of a rebellious teenager, but I told myself that looks could be deceiving. She caught me watching her and asked, "Do you know if Irma Vargas is here tonight?"

"She is," I said. "That's her at the other end of the bar."

The young woman stared at Irma, sizing her up. "She's nothing like what I expected."

Irma high-fived a customer. As if she felt our eyes on her, she turned in our direction and headed our way. She narrowed her eyes at the young woman. "What can I get you?"

"You're Irma Vargas?"

Irma tilted her head. "I am."

"My name's Zoe. Are you hiring?"

The Mermaid Cafe had been short-staffed lately, and I expected Irma to hand Zoe an application right away. Instead, she began asking questions. "Where do you live?"

Zoe hesitated. "Um, I'm looking for a place. But I kinda wanted to find a job first."

Irma must have noticed Zoe hungrily watching me sop up the last of my bisque with the French bread.

"How about some lobster bisque?" Irma suggested.

"How much is it?" she asked Irma, then lowered her eyes. "I'm, you know, on a budget."

Irma surprised me by saying, "On the house." Those were words she rarely spoke.

When she returned with the soup, Irma set it in front of Zoe and told us she'd be back in a few minutes.

"Oh em gee," Zoe gushed after the first spoonful. "This is yummylicious."

I smiled at her made-up word. "Yeah, Irma is a superb cook."

"*She* made this?"

"Her chef and the rest of the kitchen staff do most of the cooking, but she supervises. And she developed and tested all the recipes. The Mermaid Cafe is the best kept secret in Northern California."

Irma returned just as Zoe finished her last spoonful. "How old are you?"

"Um…" she began, her eyes darting from Irma to me and back again. "Twenty-one."

Irma raised an eyebrow. "And that's what your driver's license says?"

"Well, I don't have a driver's license." Zoe avoided making eye contact with either of us. "I mean, I lost it."

"How old are you?" Irma asked again. "The truth this time."

"Um…" Zoe stared at her empty bowl of soup. "Eighteen."

Irma moved on to another question. "Why are you here in Serenity Cove with no place to live and no job?"

"I, uh…" Zoe hesitated again, then shrugged. "I've always wanted to live here."

Irma came out from behind the bar and headed back toward us. Zoe watched wide-eyed as she approached us.

Irma stepped up to the young woman until they

were almost nose to nose. In a low voice so only I would hear, she said, "I don't know why you're lying, but I don't like it one bit. I want the straight scoop, and I want it now."

Her eyes wide, Zoe swallowed hard. "Um…" she began.

"Yes?" Irma prompted.

"I'm your granddaughter."

CHAPTER 2

*I*rma stared at the young woman sitting at her bar. "You're my granddaughter?"

Few people knew that Irma had given up her baby for adoption when she'd been about Zoe's age. I could almost see the wheels turning as Irma calculated how old her daughter would have been when Zoe was born.

"What proof do you have that we're related?" Irma asked. The lack of emotion in her voice surprised me, but the younger woman took it in stride.

"I took one of those online DNA tests that tell you what your ancestry is and tells you who you're related to. You took one too, so I figured you must want to find us."

Irma sighed. "I forgot about that. I took it in a moment of weakness."

I became aware we were being watched by some of Irma's other patrons. One man at the other end of the bar waved to get Irma's attention. "Why don't I take Zoe to my house, and you can come over when you're able to leave." Besides having a restaurant to run, I figured Irma could use some time to process the bombshell that had just hit her.

"That's a good idea," Irma mumbled. "Thanks."

Irma went back behind the bar and wiped down the bar.

"It's a short walk," I said as Zoe followed me outside, her knapsack slung over her shoulder. "Is that everything you have?"

"Yeah."

We walked in silence along the beach as the sun set over the ocean. The sky filled with brilliant shades of orange and purple, but Zoe stared at the ground as she walked.

"This is it." I pointed across the street, looked both ways, then crossed to my huge, pink Victorian home.

Zoe glanced at the sign above the door as we walked up the steps. "You live in a tearoom?"

"It's more like I have a tearoom in my house." I unlocked the door and held it open for her to enter. "The bedrooms are upstairs—I even have a second kitchen on the second floor, but we rarely use it."

"Wow," she said, taking in the surroundings. "It's so extra. Did you do all this yourself?"

By "this," I assumed she meant the decorating. "My assistant, Jennifer, helped. Not your taste?"

She stared up at one of the chandeliers. "Nah, it's lit."

Hoping that was a compliment, I decided to show her around. After a quick tour of the first floor, we climbed the steps and I pointed out the three bedrooms, the bathroom with the claw foot tub, and the upstairs kitchen. I explained that the house had been built as two residences before the first floor had been converted to a French restaurant.

Opening the door to the guest bathroom, I pointed out the plush towels, lotions, and toiletries. She took in everything with wide eyes.

"I might have gotten a bit carried away," I admitted. "Why don't you freshen up and I'll make us some hot cocoa. Do you like marshmallows in yours? I made some from scratch."

Her eyes lit up and she smiled for the first time since I'd met her. "That sounds…"

"Yummylicious?"

Her smile widened. "Yeah."

When Zoe came back downstairs, hot cocoa and cookies waited for her by the fire. We chatted about her school, friends, and hobbies. Her number one hobby was video games.

Eventually I got around to asking about her family, and I learned she'd been raised just outside San Diego. Her parents had been married nearly twenty-five years.

"Did you have any brothers or sisters?" I asked.

"Nope," she said. "Just me. I'm the typical only child according to my dad. He tells me all the time that I have a bad attitude."

I chuckled, and Zoe frowned, making me think of a good friend of mine. "You remind me a lot of your grandmother."

"Really?" Her eyes sparkled with hope for a moment

before she hid behind a mask of indifference. "I'm not sure she likes me."

"I'm not sure Irma likes anyone," I said playfully. "At least not at first. And I didn't much care for her when I first met her. She's like a fungus."

Zoe's face scrunched in confusion. "A fungus?"

I grinned. "She grows on you."

Instead of laughing, Zoe said, "Maybe I'm a fungus, too. I'm pretty sure that's what Dad would say."

"Sounds like you don't get along with them."

"It's just, you know… they're so different from me. Like they never understood me. They wanted me to work hard and get good grades, but all I ever wanted to do was draw and paint. There's good jobs if you're good at art. Like maybe I could work on video games."

"That's a fantastic idea."

"Video games are a waste of time." She shrugged. "That's what they always said."

"Sorry they didn't get it."

"They didn't get me," Zoe said. "I used to want to shake my mom and tell her there's more to life than working and housework and watching TV every night."

My curiosity about Irma's daughter finally got the better of me. "What's your mother like?"

"Mom's okay, I guess. She's not that much taller than…" She hesitated as if not sure what to call Irma. "She's only five foot two. I look more like my dad. But I really don't think I take after either of them."

"They know where you are, right?"

"Oh, sure." She didn't make eye contact with me, but

before I could press the question, my phone buzzed with a text from Irma.

Zoe must have seen me frown. "Is something wrong?"

"Irma had a late rush and she's not sure how soon she can leave." Seeing Zoe's disappointed expression, I explained, "They're really short staffed right now. This is such a small town and during the off season it's hard to find people willing to drive from Somerton or other neighboring towns to work a five or six-hour shift."

Zoe set her cup on a coaster on the table, her eyes downcast. "Maybe I should leave." She took a deep breath and let it out slowly. "Maybe coming here was a bad idea."

"Not at all." I patted her arm. "You showing up here was a huge surprise for Irma. I don't think she even knew she had a grandchild."

She stared into her cup, blinking back tears. "Yeah, you're probably right."

"She just needs a little time to get used to the idea. I think you should know that Irma's not someone who's —how should I put this? She's never going to be a 'hugging and cookie baking' kind of grandmother."

Zoe nodded. "Yeah, I get that."

"But she's as loyal and good-hearted as they come. Once she gets used to your purple hair and tattoos and you get used to her snark, I bet you'll get along great."

"Yeah, right," she mumbled, her voice flat.

I doubted she believed me. "Why don't you spend the night here? I've got a guest room ready to go."

Before she could object, I added, "It'll be no trouble at all."

"Really?" She looked at me with wide, innocent eyes. "If you're totally sure…"

"I'll text Irma and let her know. She can come over in the morning and you two can start getting to know each other. You have a lot of catching up to do."

At that moment, I heard a key in the back door, and moments later, Jennifer pushed open the door from the kitchen.

"You're still up?" She stopped when she saw I wasn't alone. "Oh, hello."

"This is Zoe, Irma's granddaughter," I said. "She's staying the night."

Jennifer pursed her lips. "Irma has a granddaughter?"

"She does now." I stood, ready to carry our cups into the kitchen.

Jennifer headed for the staircase. She stopped and tipped her head to one side. "Is she staying in the guest room?"

"Yes, of course," I said. "Would you mind taking her upstairs and showing her where everything is?"

"Sure!" Jennifer paused with one foot on the bottom step. "Wait till you see it, Zoe. It's so extra—you're going to love it."

THE NEXT MORNING, I FOUND JENNIFER AND ZOE chatting up a storm in the kitchen. Chef was nowhere to be seen. Jennifer jumped up the moment I entered and hurried to the cappuccino machine.

"You don't have to do that," I said as I did almost every morning.

Jennifer flipped switches on the machine and began doing her magic. "Oh, yes I do." In a loud aside to Zoe, she said, "She's barely fit to be around until she has her first cup of coffee."

"Hey, I can hear you, you know." I pretended to scowl before telling Zoe in a loud whisper, "She's not wrong."

Before I could ask Zoe what she'd like for breakfast, my phone buzzed. I picked it up from the charger and looked at the screen. It was a text from Sheriff Fontana.

Anyone ask you for dirt on me?

That seemed odd. I answered, *no, why?* and waited for a response.

A minute later, it came: *Practice saying no comment.*

Jennifer must have seen the puzzled look on my face because she asked, "What's up?"

I shook my head, though I wasn't sure one way or the other. "I'm sure it's nothing. Are you a big breakfast eater?" I asked Zoe. "I can make bacon and eggs."

She smiled shyly. "I'm vegan."

"Oh." I tried to think what I could throw together on short notice that didn't include eggs or milk. I had a few vegan dishes for the tearoom guests who requested them, but soup, salad, or chickpea stew didn't sound like appealing breakfast choices.

"Just coffee is fine for me," Zoe said. "Jennifer made me a latte with oat milk."

"I know—pancakes!" I'd seen a recipe that used oat milk and replaced the eggs with oil. "We have more oat milk, right?"

"Sure do." Jennifer opened the refrigerator to retrieve it.

Zoe blurted out, "Please don't make them just for me. I don't want to be any trouble."

"No trouble at all. I've been wanting to try the recipe but didn't have a reason until now." I got out the mixing bowl and pulled up the recipe on my phone. "I love experimenting."

Jennifer winked at Zoe. "Her experiments are almost always edible, too."

Chef shimmered into view. "Bah! The culinary arts are a science, not a mishmash of guessing and experimentation."

I wanted to tell him that science involved a lot of experimentation too, but as usual, having company in the kitchen required me to stay silent.

Zoe's shoulders relaxed as she watched me worked. I wanted to make her feel at home, and nothing said welcome like a warm scone or a stack of vegan pancakes.

"Did anyone in your family teach you to bake?" I asked Zoe as I set the batter aside to rest and turned on the burner under the stove's built-in griddle.

"I wasn't allowed in the kitchen much." She grimaced. "I've always been really clumsy—spilling stuff or breaking things."

"Really? Me, too." Jennifer opened the oven and pointed inside. "See the silicone guards on the edge of the racks? April bought them after I burned myself for about the hundredth time. And she stopped giving me the really nice teacups. I kept breaking them."

"You only broke one, as I recall." It was one of my favorites, but I left that unsaid.

Jennifer grinned. "It gets me out of doing dishes by hand. April washes the dainty dishes, and I just load the dishwasher."

Jennifer took a seat next to Zoe at the island. An alert pinged on my phone from the city council, and I read it as the two young women chatted. The recall committee had scheduled a press conference on the steps of city hall for later that afternoon. It seemed odd that they were holding it in our little town, but maybe they wanted to start off small and move to the bigger towns later.

I glanced over at Zoe, who seemed content to listen to Jennifer tell her about her favorite subjects, which happened to be history, antiques, and historic clothing.

"Want to come up and see my costume collection?" Jennifer asked. The two young women scrambled up the back staircase to the second floor.

Since it was a new recipe, I started with a single pancake to see if I'd need to make any modifications. Pouring a scoop of batter onto the griddle, I watched as bubbles slowly began to form and pop. When the surface looked as bumpy as the lunar surface, I flipped it.

My annoyance with Irma grew as the minutes ticked by and she hadn't shown up. Didn't she want to spend time with her granddaughter? Maybe she was still recovering from her shock.

As if she knew I'd been thinking about her, Irma entered through the back door dressed in khaki shorts and a floppy hat. She leaned her walking stick against the counter.

"Good morning," she said cheerily as if it were a normal day. Except that it wasn't a normal day and Irma rarely was cheerful. She preferred to maintain her reputation as the town's curmudgeon. She looked around the kitchen. "Where is everyone?"

Before I could answer, Jennifer came clomping down the back stairs. Zoe, right behind her, froze in her tracks.

"I'm making pancakes," I announced, hoping to lighten the mood, leaving out the fact that they were vegan. Irma often objected to my attempts at healthy cooking. "Trying out a new recipe. They'll be ready in a jiffy."

"Sounds great." Irma stood near the back door as if not sure what to do next.

I looked from Irma to Zoe. "On second thought, the pancakes can wait. I'll let you two talk." Removing the single pancake from the griddle and setting it on a plate, I headed for the door to the front room. Jennifer got the hint and turned to follow me.

"No, no, no," Irma said, sounding more like her usual self. "You two are like family. I'd like you to stay while I get to know my actual family." She pulled up a stool at the island and gestured to another stool. "Have a seat, Zoe."

Jennifer made Irma a mocha latte and for a few moments no one talked over the hissing cappuccino machine. I took a bite of the pancake to test how it came out and grimaced. After a second bite to make sure, I tossed it. They were nice and fluffy but flavorless, and I didn't think maple syrup would do enough to fix that.

"So," Irma began once the noise died down, "I didn't know I had a granddaughter, so I hope you can forgive my reaction last night. Not that you have to forgive me, but…"

"No worries." Zoe shrugged. "I didn't know I had a grandma until a couple of weeks ago. I mean, I had grandparents, but I didn't even know my mom was adopted. All my grandparents are gone now. They were really old." She stopped talking abruptly. "Sorry. Sometimes I talk too much."

"No way," Jennifer told Zoe as she set down the mocha she'd just made.

Irma's mouth twitched at the sight of the heart Jennifer had created in the foam. "I always thought one day your mom might show up out of the blue the way you did. For years, I rehearsed what I'd say if she did, playing out every possible scenario in my mind."

"What would you have said to her?" Zoe asked.

Irma took a sip of her drink before answering. "I'd like to know if she's had a good life. Has she?"

Zoe scrunched up her face as if faced with a difficult math problem. "Yeah… I guess so."

"So, she's happy?" Irma asked.

"Um… probably not." Zoe sighed. "But is anyone really happy?"

"I am," I interjected. "Happy, that is."

"Me, too," Jennifer added. "Most of the time, anyway."

We all looked at Irma.

She didn't answer right away. "I'm content, I suppose," she finally said. "I was bitter for a long, long time after I gave up your mom for adoption. I think you're old enough to hear the story. If you want." When Zoe nodded, Irma continued. "I was engaged to a wonderful man—or at least I thought he was wonderful. Then the woman who used to own this house stole him away from me. They got married and I left town to have my baby. As soon as she was born, I gave her up for adoption." She hung her head. "Things were different then. I could barely support myself, much less a baby."

I felt Chef's presence behind me and turned to watch him.

His blue eyes questioned me. "This cannot be true."

Since I couldn't say anything out loud unless I wanted to choose this moment to finally tell Jennifer about Chef and explain to Zoe I had a ghost in my kitchen, I nodded and got back to my dilemma with the pancakes. As I was about to toss the batter and start over, I remembered I'd bought too many blueberries on sale and froze what I didn't use. After retrieving them from the freezer, I tossed about a cup into the batter and folded them in.

Dropping some water on the griddle, I watched it

skip across the surface. That meant the temperature was perfect.

"Norma stole Irma's fiancé from her?" Chef asked. "And Irma was with child?"

I smiled at his old-fashioned language and nodded again as I used a quarter cup measure to scoop pancake batter onto the griddle.

"I cannot believe I was in love with such a person," Chef said. "Such a horrible person."

Everyone jumped as the door to the back room flew open. A cold breeze rushed into the kitchen and the lights flickered. I gave Chef a warning look. He should know better than to insult Norma, especially when we had company.

CHAPTER 3

After I'd locked the back door to prevent it flying open again, I returned to the pancakes in time to hear Irma ask Zoe, "How old are you *really?*"

Zoe sighed, and for a moment I thought she'd stick with her previous answer. Instead, she said, "I'm seventeen. But I'll be eighteen in two months."

"Does your mother know where you are?" Irma demanded.

"Sort of," Zoe said, sulking.

"What does that mean?" Irma asked. When Zoe didn't answer, she demanded, "Call her. Now."

While Zoe squirmed in her chair, I nearly burned the pancakes, flipping them over just in time.

"Where's your phone?" Irma did her best to sound calm and forgiving, but I heard the stress in her voice as she tried to control her temper.

"Can I text her?" Zoe asked.

"Call." Irma's tone said she wasn't taking no for an answer.

Zoe seemed to accept the inevitable and pulled out her phone. After several more sighs, she made the call.

Not wanting to intrude, I transferred the pancakes to a platter and turned the fire off under the griddle. With a quick gesture to Jennifer, I stepped into the front room, and she followed close behind.

"Wow," Jennifer said as the door swung closed behind us.

I stayed close to the door, my curiosity fighting with my desire to give Irma and Zoe their privacy. "Should I start a fire?"

Jennifer stood next to me as faint voices came from the kitchen. "I think it's going to be warm today." Jennifer pulled out her phone, and a moment later gave me a weather report. "It says the high will be seventy-two degrees."

"My favorite temperature. No more rain?"

"Not today. At least not in the forecast, but if you go out, I'd take an umbrella just in case."

Zoe's voice floated through the door. "But Mom." After a pause, we heard her say. "Why don't you talk to her? She's right here."

Feeling guilty for eavesdropping, I weaved through the tearoom tables to the window overlooking the front yard. I wanted to see what the day looked like for myself. Across the street, beyond the sidewalk and short beach, waves crashed lazily against the shore. Fluffy cotton candy clouds floated by in a bright blue sky. The gorgeous scene in front of me didn't distract me from wondering how Zoe's and Irma's conversation was going in the kitchen.

Jennifer appeared next to me, speaking in a hushed tone. "I wish I knew what was going on in there. Do you think Irma's daughter is going to be ticked off at Zoe for coming here and not telling her? Maybe she'll blame Irma. Which is not fair at all. After all, Irma knew nothing about it until last night. Oh! Do you think Zoe's mom will drive to Serenity Cove to get her?"

I smiled at Jennifer's run-on one-way conversation. "It's sweet that you're nervous for Irma."

"Nervous? I'm not..." She smiled shyly. "Okay, I'm freaking out. Why aren't you?"

I chuckled. "Wait until you get to be my age. Or Irma's age. You either learn not to freak out or at least not show it. Sometimes a little of both."

The kitchen door swung open, and Irma poked her head out. "You can come back in. Everything's settled."

Jennifer and I returned to the kitchen. After turning the griddle back on, I served the first batch of blueberry pancakes to Zoe and Irma. She pronounced them delicious, and even Irma agreed. The blueberries had saved the day, and maple syrup didn't hurt.

Irma wiped some syrup off her chin. "We'll have to figure out what you're going to do when I'm at the Mermaid Cafe. You can't come and work with me," Irma said. "Not for a few more months, anyway. My servers have to be at least eighteen."

"I could work in the kitchen. I'll wash dishes."

Irma narrowed her eyes. "You wouldn't last a week. It's hard work."

Zoe sat up straight on her stool. "I'm not afraid of hard work."

I interrupted their little spat before it escalated. "You can come over here in the evening if you want, Zoe. You're always welcome."

Jennifer piped up. "You can always watch me study."

"It's more exciting than it sounds," I said.

Jennifer giggled. "No, it's really not."

Irma stared at a tattoo just above Zoe's wrist peeking out from her long-sleeve shirt. "Don't you have to get your parents' permission to get a tattoo when you're under eighteen?"

Zoe squirmed in her seat. "I lied about my age."

"Uh, huh." Irma licked her thumb then reached for Zoe's arm.

I held my breath, not sure what she was doing. She rubbed at the tattoo then held up her black thumb for me to see.

"They're fake?" I hadn't suspected—how had Irma known?

Irma began to laugh. "I got a fake tattoo when I was around your age. I got grounded for a week, and I still never admitted it was fake." She shook her head. "Looks like you're a chip off the old block."

I turned my eyes to the ceiling. "Heaven help us."

Irma told Zoe to get her things so they could go home. The younger woman grinned and hurried up the stairs.

As soon as she was out of earshot, I asked, "So what happened? Did you talk to your daughter?"

Irma stared at her empty plate shaking her head slowly. "Suzanne. It's a nice name, don't you think?"

"She didn't want to talk to you?"

"She's not ready." Irma's eyes shone with emotion. "It's just as well. I'm not sure I'm ready either. But at least she's agreed to let Zoe stay with me for a while. I get the feeling they could use a break from each other."

"Not unusual when it comes to teenagers. But what about—"

"Everything else can wait." Irma's tone, stern and solid, told me the rest of my questions would have to remain unanswered for now.

~

The recall campaign's press conference was scheduled for three o'clock. Around two, I drove to city hall, hoping to speak with Deputy Alex Molina, our acting police chief. Molina acted as the only law enforcement officer in our little town during the off season—in summer, when the town's population ballooned with tourists, the county assigned a second deputy to assist him.

Entering city hall, I walked past the empty information desk and down a long walk past the mayor's office. I hoped I wouldn't run into the mayor, who'd been a thorn in my side since I'd first met her. To be fair, she probably felt the same about me.

I pulled open the police station door and entered.

No one occupied the reception desk, so I walked past it to Molina's office and knocked on his door.

A voice much lower than Molina's answered back, "Come in."

I opened the door and found the imposing figure of Sheriff Anderson Fontana behind the desk—tall and handsome. He was also married, which didn't stop the butterflies in my stomach whenever I saw him. The baby-faced Deputy Molina stood next to him, his dark hair ruffled as always. Neither looked surprised to see me, but then, they both were good at hiding their true feelings. I supposed it was necessary in their line of work.

"Hello, Deputy," I said, greeting Molina first. "Hello, Sheriff."

"I'll be right with you," Fontana replied before turning to Molina. "We have five other deputies arriving at fourteen-thirty for reinforcements—just in case there's any trouble. Not that I expect any."

Molina nodded. "And you'll be directing them?"

"You're in charge today." As he spoke, Fontana gathered the papers on the desk into a neat stack. "I'm planning to stay here in your office out of sight. My presence would only be a distraction."

Molina glanced at me, then back at the sheriff. "I'll wait in the other room." He walked past me without making eye contact and closed the door behind him.

I took a seat across from Fontana. "What's going on?"

He leaned back in his chair and crossed his arms over his chest. "Nice to see you too, Ms. May. It's been a while. You haven't found another dead body, have you?"

I smirked to let him know I didn't find his comment funny. "You don't think this recall is a real threat, do you? From what everyone says, you've been doing a great job and you're really popular, at least in Serenity Cove."

"That's good to hear, but we'll see if that's still the case after the press conference."

"What could they possibly say that would..." My mind searched for a credible reason Fontana's career might be at risk. "Does he have something on you?" Did our fine, upstanding sheriff have a secret that his political enemies planned to use against him? A thought popped into my head. "Or is this about your wife?"

Sheriff smiled grimly. "A lot of people weren't happy when the D.A. didn't prosecute her for covering up her friend's husband's murder."

I raised my hand. "Like me. I had more reason than anyone to be furious about her getting off with nothing more than a slap on the hand. Her so-called friend nearly killed me. I didn't *necessarily* want Cheryl to go to prison, but it seemed wrong that there were no repercussions for her. Why should she get off scot-free just because she agreed to testify?"

"That's how the system works, sometimes. We have to make deals to make sure the bad guys go to prison. And stay there." The sheriff grimaced. "But you're wrong to say she's not suffering any consequences. She was forced off the board of Maynard Industries, the company her father founded. He's the CEO and had been grooming her to be his successor for years. That's off the table after the scandal."

"Oh, boo hoo." I could tell my remark stung, but I had trouble being sympathetic.

"I hear the recall committee is looking for volunteers," he said wryly.

"I'll admit I'm bitter, but not *that* bitter. Besides, I don't blame you." The sheriff wasn't responsible for his wife's poor decisions. "I do feel bad if the 'scandal' as you call it, keeps you from being reelected."

"That might not be the only thing they're planning to use against me. I've learned through my sources that one of the committee members is trying to dig up dirt on me."

"But if you have nothing else to hide…" *Other than a scheming wife.*

"No, but…" The sheriff straightened up in his seat and sucked in a breath. He let it out slowly before saying, "Cheryl has asked me for a divorce."

"Oh." That was the last thing I expect him to say. Even though I had a suspicion they had a marriage in name only, Fontana would have stuck with his wife to the bitter end no matter how miserable he was.

He gave me a wry smile. "I can tell you're not shedding any tears over it."

"But you are? It didn't take a psychic to know you weren't happy, even before recent events."

He stared past me, as if lost in the past. "I was so in love with her. She was so beautiful—still is." He paused before going on. "But that's not why I fell in love with her. She was so full of life, ready to take on the world head on. We were going to make a difference together —as a team." His voice caught. He cleared his throat and continued. "Cheryl has agreed to wait until after the election to file. But of course, her friends know. It probably won't surprise you that I don't trust them not to share that information."

I had little respect for Cheryl's friends, sure they would sell her out in a heartbeat. "But getting a divorce is hardly a shameful secret these days. Would people actually vote against you for that? After everything you've done for our county?"

"Probably not," Fontana said. "But I don't think the recall committee will leave it at that."

"What do you mean?"

"There's a rumor about another woman. And I think they plan to capitalize on that rumor by spreading it around while pretending to have nothing to do with it."

I didn't believe for a moment that Fontana had cheated on Cheryl. "Who's this other woman supposed to be?"

"You."

CHAPTER 4

"*M*e?" I stared at the sheriff in disbelief. "Someone thinks that you and I—?" I couldn't finish the thought—it was too ridiculous. Sure, I'd felt an attraction to the sheriff, but I would never have admitted it to him or anyone else.

"I know it's a load of hooey, but you remember when Cheryl had us followed last year?"

"How could I forget?" I'd thought someone was after me, and the whole time it was just some third-rate private investigator his wife had hired.

"Somehow, that information got out. I think a reporter bribed the PI, but since there wasn't anything to back up the story, the newspaper never printed it."

My thoughts whirled, remembering people giving me funny looks over the past few weeks. Did people really think I was a home wrecker? Middle-aged, ordinary me?

"And considering the rumor," Fontana continued, "I'd suggest we avoid being seen together."

"Oh, right." I stood. "I guess I should leave now then."

"April?"

I turned back. "Yes?"

The sheriff, always so strong and rugged, seemed deflated somehow. "I'm sorry it had to end this way."

I walked through the outer office past Deputy Molina while wondering what the sheriff meant by his comment. I'd begun to consider Sheriff Fontana a friend, someone who I could rely on in a crisis. His words told me I couldn't count on him for help in the future—but as long as no one else got murdered, I wouldn't need his assistance. And as for our budding friendship, I told myself I had plenty of other friends.

Once outside, I made my way to the front of the building where workers busied themselves setting up for the press conference. A podium with a microphone stood at the top of the steps facing the street. A number of people milled about on the sidewalk, and I felt their eyes watching me.

"Don't be paranoid," I mumbled to myself, thinking it might be best if I left, but curious to hear what the speaker had to say. Before I could make up my mind, Irma grabbed my arm.

"What are you doing here?" she hissed.

"What are you talking about?" I asked, although I had a feeling I knew the answer. "There's going to be a press conference. You're here. Why shouldn't I be?"

She seemed to realize she'd said too much. "No reason," she answered, a little too casually.

I lowered my voice to just above a whisper. "Irma

Vargas, you know about the rumors about Sheriff Fontana and me." I waited for her to try to deny it, but she said nothing. "And you didn't think to tell me?"

She dismissed my question with a wave of her hand. "I knew it wasn't true. Why upset you?"

"Maybe," I said under my breath, "so I wouldn't be ten times as upset right now with all these people around."

The crowd had grown, and we did our best to blend in. It was especially easy for Irma, since she stood barely five feet tall. I hunched down, hoping to be less conspicuous.

"Where's Zoe?" I asked, wondering why her granddaughter wasn't with her.

"I dropped her off at the mall in Somerton with some money for new outfits. She brought hardly anything with her."

My heart warmed thinking of Irma wasting no time to start spoiling Zoe. "Why didn't you stay with her and help her pick out clothes?"

She gave me a "are you an idiot?" look. "When you were seventeen, would you have wanted your grandmother helping you choose your wardrobe?" She paused long enough to see my reaction. "That's what I thought. Besides, I wanted to see what the recall committee has up its sleeve. When this is over, I'll drive back and pick her up."

A man of about thirty with a neatly trimmed beard walked up to the podium. His bright, royal blue suit assured that all eyes were on him as he checked the microphone.

I leaned closer to Irma and said, "Who's that? He looks like an actor."

"Looks like they hired a pretty boy to run the recall campaign."

A woman in front of us turned and shushed us. Her eyes widened when she saw me. I barely restrained myself from sticking my tongue out at her. Had everyone in town heard the rumor about the sheriff and me?

The man at the podium began to speak, his voice booming and full of enthusiasm. "Good afternoon. My name is Ray Quimby, and I'm leading the effort to remove Sheriff Anderson Fontana from office." Polite applause came from the crowd, along with a number of boos.

I scanned the crowd closest to the podium and spotted Chief Deputy Rugger. In his uniform, Rugger reminded me of a drill sergeant with his muscular shoulders and buzz cut. I guessed him to be in his late thirties or early forties, which would make him a few years younger than Sheriff Fontana.

Quimby spoke enthusiastically about Serenity Cove and the other towns in our county. Despite his public speaking skills and booming voice, the crowd began mumbling and a few people wandered off. He must have realized he was losing the crowd, because he slammed a hand on the podium.

"Enough about the past." He paused meaningfully. "Sheriff Fontana is not qualified to be your sheriff any longer. A sheriff must have high moral character. Can Sheriff Fontana claim to be beyond reproach?"

A few members of the crowd shouted out, "Yes!" while others shouted, "No!" More people began to yell and someone behind me shoved me into the woman standing in front of me.

"Hey!" she shouted, then added, "This is all your fault."

"*My* fault? What are you talking about?" I yelled back.

Irma grabbed me by the elbow and dragged me away from the crowd toward the parking lot, not stopping until we reached my car.

"Why'd you pull me away?" I asked. "I wasn't done with her. How dare she suggest…"

"I wanted to keep you off the front page of the newspaper," Irma huffed. "But if you'd like to go back and duke it out with some idiot, be my guest."

I took a deep breath before deciding to listen to reason. "Let's go."

CHAPTER 5

*A*fter returning home, I warmed up some leftover soup for an early dinner. I looked up the phone number and address of the recall campaign headquarters in Somerton. No one answered the phone. It was nearly five p.m., and it occurred to me they might have closed for the day. Too impatient to wait for the morning, I got in my car and headed out to see Quimby. I wanted to find out what information he'd dug up in case I needed to correct him on any rumors involving me. As a business owner and community member, I had a reputation to protect, after all.

When I arrived in Somerton less than half an hour later, the streets were nearly empty—like most of the small towns in our county, they rolled up the sidewalks at five. Hopefully, Quimby hadn't closed their offices and gone home.

My GPS system directed me to turn on a small side street, and I scanned the shops, looking for Rugger's headquarters. Time seemed to have forgotten the street lined with dingy-looking shops: a vacuum cleaner repair shop, a dry cleaner, and a barber, all with signs that appeared fifty years old or more.

The GPS told me I'd arrived at my destination. "Where?" I gazed at a faded sign that said, "Miller's Carpets." Taking a second look, I saw a banner hung in the window proclaiming, "Recall Sheriff Fontana."

I found a parking spot a few doors down and checked the parking meter. Every shop was closed, but I still had to pay to park until six p.m. After digging in my purse for quarters and coming up empty, I felt thankful that unlike the shops, the meter had been upgraded. I swiped my credit card to give me an hour of time, plenty of time to give Quimby a piece of my mind.

Peering around painted flags and posters hung in the windows, the interior appeared lifeless. I twisted the doorknob and entered a small dingy room stepping on ancient, brown linoleum tile.

"Hello?" My voice echoed in the nearly empty space.

Three gray, metal desks faced the front with a file cabinet and some tables lining the back wall. I approached the largest desk in the center of the room. Papers cluttered the desktop, and I picked up one—a printout of an email. I chuckled to myself. It was usually the older generation who printed emails, and I was pretty sure Quimby was at least a decade younger than me.

The email turned out to be a confirmation for a

bank transfer for a total of several thousand dollars. I read the name on the account: Ray Quimby.

After calling out "Hello," again, I pulled out my phone and took a picture of the email. If Ray wanted to keep his emails private, then he shouldn't go leaving them lying around in plain view.

It seemed odd that he hadn't locked up when he left for the day, but maybe he'd just stepped out to grab a cup of coffee. While I waited, what harm would there be in taking a look around?

As I made my way to the back of the small room, where stacks of papers were strewn on one of the tables. I picked up a flyer which had an unflattering picture of Fontana unshaven in an old T-shirt. It listed several unsubstantiated claims including "questionable handling of city funds," "soft on crime," and "moral turpitude."

"Now, that's going too far," I muttered, not at all sure what "moral turpitude" meant. It sounded like a serious accusation, nonetheless.

While I glanced at the other flyers, all with a similar theme, I pondered whether to wait any longer. I might as well do some shopping in town and return later. As I turned to leave, I sucked in a breath.

Ray Quimby lay on the floor behind his desk, a large, red stain on his white shirt.

CHAPTER 6

I dropped the flyer and rushed to his side, pulling out my phone to call the paramedics.

"Don't be dead. Don't be dead," I muttered as I pressed my fingers to the side of his neck, then checked his wrist.

A woman's voice came on the line. "What is your emergency?"

"A man is…" Not wanting to say the word, "dead," I took a deep breath and started again. "I think he's been shot." I checked his neck again for a pulse, but the dark stain on his shirt told me it was too late. "There's no pulse and I think… I think he's dead." My head felt light and I reached for the desk chair and sat down.

While I spoke to the operator, I couldn't take my gaze off Quimby's motionless figure. I found my eyes drawn to his right hand and a dark red stain on the tip of his index finger. Inches away from his hand, something had been written on the floor. It appeared to be the letter "R" followed by an incoherent smear, and I felt sure it had been written in blood.

The front door opened, and I spun around in the chair to see a tall man in uniform with muscular shoulders and a buzz cut. He looked familiar, somehow. I guessed him to be in his late thirties or early forties

"You were quick," I said stupidly.

"Who are you?" he asked.

"April May. Who are you?"

"Chief Deputy Arthur Rugger."

I spoke into the phone. "The chief deputy is here."

He narrowed his eyes at me. "What's going on here?"

My eyes drifted back to Quimby's body lying on the floor. "I'm pretty sure he's dead."

In a few long strides, Rugger reached Quimby and dropped to his knees. After checking his vitals, he grabbed the phone from me. I felt reassured to know that someone as competent and experienced as the Chief Deputy had arrived to take care of everything.

That feeling was short-lived.

Once he'd done everything he could for Quimby, he began barking questions at me, starting with, "Who are you?"

"I'm April May."

"Oh, is that so." He nodded knowingly. "What are you doing here? Did you decide to branch out to Somerton? I always knew there was something suspicious about you. Where is Krissyanne?"

"Who?"

"I'll ask the questions here." As he continued to grill me, I didn't like the direction he was headed.

"Did you come to confront Quimby?" he asked. "Were you going to pay him off to keep quiet? Is that why you killed him—because he wouldn't take your bribe? You had to shut him up somehow. Where's the gun?"

As I did my best to answer, I struggled to focus on something calming. As soon as I got home, I'd make a nice cup of hot tea. Maybe the new wildflower blend I hadn't had a chance to try yet. And all the shortbread cookies I could eat.

"Are you even listening to me?" he demanded.

Fed up with his attitude, I stood and put my hands on my hips. "Why should I? You've obviously decided that I shot Quimby. Why not read me my rights and take me off to jail? You might even be able to make it home in time for dinner."

Rugger narrowed his eyes accusingly. "I don't need your smart mouth, Miss May."

Sirens approached, distracting Rugger from his interrogation of me. Soon, the paramedics rushed in, and I stepped aside to give them room to work.

Two sheriff's deputies arrived, a man and a woman, both of whom looked very young. The chief deputy gave them instructions in a low voice as if he wanted to make sure I didn't overhear. Feeling woozy, I took a few steps toward a chair.

"You're not going anywhere," Rugger called out to me.

Frustration and anger began replacing my feelings

of shock and disbelief. Rugger instructed one of the deputies to swab me for GSR, which I knew meant gunshot residue.

I felt the room begin to spin.

One of the paramedics pushed a chair over to me and eased me into it. "How are you feeling?" she asked.

"I'm not sure." I looked at her face. "You have pretty eyes. They're gray."

"Yes, they are," she said with a kind smile. "I'm going to take your blood pressure just to make sure it's normal. Is that okay?"

I nodded. While she wrapped the cuff around my arm and pumped it, the male deputy asked me to hold out my hands to be swabbed.

"Can't you wait a minute?" Gray Eyes groused.

When everyone had finished with me, I looked up to see a welcome face. Dr. Fredeline Severs, the county coroner and my friend, had arrived. With her focus on the dead body, she didn't notice me right away. I watched her work, marveling at her competence and how she took the circumstances in stride.

How many dead bodies would I have to see before it became routine for me? I hoped to never find out.

Freddie's eyes widened when she saw me. "Excuse me, Chief Deputy?" she called out to Rugger. "What is Ms. May doing here?"

He closed the distance between them in moments. He leaned close to her, speaking quietly. I didn't hear what he said, but I heard Freddie's response.

"A suspect?" Freddie's voice was incredulous. "You're kidding, right?"

Rugger scowled. "You do your job, Dr. Severs, and I'll do mine. Have you determined time of death?"

Her eyes narrowed at his comment, but her demeanor remained professional. "Sometime between four and five o'clock based on—"

"It couldn't have been later?" he interrupted. "Say, seventeen-thirty."

She stared at him for a long moment. "That seems unlikely." She stood. "I'll know more when I get him to the morgue."

"Twenty minutes after the hour, perhaps."

Freddie lowered her voice. "I'm not going to adjust my findings in order to make them fit into your predetermined theory of what happened here this evening, Chief Deputy."

Rugger head pulled back reacting to her implication. "Of course not, Dr. Severs, and I would never ask you to. I'd just like to make sure we aren't eliminating any suspects prematurely based on the time that Quimby was shot."

"Have you ever cut yourself shaving?" Freddie asked.

Rugger raised an eyebrow. "Yes, of course."

"When you dab a tissue on the cut, the blood is bright red. It begins to slowly darken the longer it's exposed to air. The hemoglobin breaks down—"

"I know about hemoglobin," Rugger cut her short. "I'm not an idiot."

"Glad to hear it," Freddie said without a trace of sarcasm. "Then you'll understand why, based on my visual inspection, I was able to quickly ascertain that the victim had been deceased for at least forty to fifty minutes, possibly more. I then confirmed my estimate by various other methods and will continue to do so when I'm able to do a more thorough examination. Would you like me to go into more detail, Chief Deputy?"

"That won't be necessary," he grumbled, then strode over to me. "What time did you arrive at this location, Ms. May?"

"A little after five-thirty," I said, relieved that the timeline alone would rule me out as a suspect. Not to mention the fact that I had no motive and no weapon.

"Anyone who can confirm your movements this evening?" he asked.

Impatience and fatigue got the better of me. "You think I shot Quimby and then just hung around for half an hour or more before I decided to call for help?"

"If you would just answer the question, please—can anyone confirm your whereabouts for the past hour or so?"

"No," I said, thinking back on the last couple of hours. "I drove here from home in Serenity Cove, parked on the street, and..." The parking meter! "Oh—I put my credit card into the meter when I arrived. So, unless I shot Mr. Quimby, got rid of the gun, then went and put money in the meter, and then came back and called for help..." That didn't sound all that improbable as I was saying it. "Can you track the location of my phone over that time? Or—I know—I bet Somerton has cameras that take pictures of every car's license plate as they enter town."

"Let me worry about how I go about verifying your alibi, Ms. May. We'll get your contact information and then you can go."

He gestured to a female deputy whose dark hair had been pulled up into a no-nonsense bun. She approached us, led me to one of the desks, and pushed a chair in my direction, introducing herself as Deputy Yolanda Lopez.

The deputy got right to business, asking me for my identification. I handed her my driver's license.

After taking down my address, phone number, and email, she said, "We'll contact you in the next day or two to get your statement."

I stood to leave when a woman in jeans and a T-shirt burst into the room, clutching a child by the hand. Strands of brown hair escaped from her messy ponytail. "What's going on? Why is there an ambulance outside?"

In two strides, Rugger stood in front of her. "There's been a tragedy, Krissyanne."

Krissyanne let go of the little girl's hand and approached Quimby's desk. The girl, about five years old, began to wail.

Instinctively, I kneeled down next to her and said, "Hi, my name's April. What's yours?"

The girl stared at me. She didn't answer, but at least she forgot to cry for the moment.

I heard Rugger softly say to Krissyanne, "Quimby has been shot."

Her mouth fell open and she placed her hands on

Rugger's chest as if to brace herself. "Shot? What do you mean? Is he going to be okay?"

Rugger shook his head slowly, and the woman fell into his arms, sobbing, her ponytail covering the lower part of her face. His eyes expressed discomfort at the public display of emotion.

The little girl stared at Krissyanne, not understanding what was going on.

"It looks like your mom is upset," I said.

In a little girl voice, the child said, "She's not my mommy."

"Oh, okay. Is she your nanny?" I asked.

Before the girl could answer, Krissyanne grabbed the girl's hand. "I need to take her home," she announced, then swooped out the door.

"Is that Quimby's wife?" I asked Deputy Lopez in a whisper.

"That's Krissyanne Dobbins. She works for the recall campaign."

"I see." I watched Krissyanne through the window as she hurried out of view. "Now that Quimby's dead, I wonder if she'll be in charge."

The deputy said, "You're free to go."

I could take a hint. With one last look at the recall office, now a crime scene, I stepped out into the dark, chilly night and turned toward my car.

Had Krissyanne wanted the job of managing the recall campaign? Would she have resorted to murder to get it?

There were people who had killed for less.

CHAPTER 7

reddie followed me out onto the dark sidewalk, calling after me. "April, wait. I shouldn't be too much longer. I'll give you a ride home."

"I don't want to leave my car here and have to come back for it."

"It'll be fine," she insisted. "I'll drive you back in the morning. You've had a shock, and I think it's better—"

"I'm okay, really. I mean, it's not the first dead body I've seen." I reached out my arms for a hug, and Freddie wrapped her arms around me tightly before letting go and returning to the crime scene.

Before getting on the highway back to Serenity Cove, I stopped at a coffee house nearby for a decaf latte and a chocolate chip cookie to help calm me. Chocolate always had that effect on me.

I considered calling Irma on my way home, but I knew how busy she was, especially now that she had her granddaughter staying with her. The twenty-five-minute drive felt endless, and I couldn't wait to get home where I'd feel safe and be able to tell Jennifer all about my evening. When I pulled into my driveway, only the porch light greeted me from the dark house. My spirits deflated. Looked like I'd be spending the evening alone.

In spite of it being nearly spring, the evening temperature had dropped into the low fifties, and I couldn't wait to get inside and start a fire. I pulled my car to the end of the driveway to take a peek at the secret garden project, hoping it would cheer me up. A quarter moon cast an eerie glow on the piles of rocks and the beginnings of a wall. At the rate George was going, I wondered if the walls would be up before summer. I had hoped to start planting by June so we could host events over the summer.

As I took in the scene, George's helper appeared.

I'd heard people talk about time standing still, but I thought they were being poetic or fanciful. The man smiled at me, his eyes twinkling. Tan and rugged, with salt and pepper hair, he held one of the boulders as if it were as light as a feather. He set it down and his lips moved.

"Excuse me?" I hadn't heard a word he said.

"You must be April May," he repeated, his voice low and husky. "I apologize for not introducing myself sooner. I'm Levi." His musical voice made me lightheaded.

Maybe I was under a spell. "Nice to meet you." *It's not polite to stare.* "Um, I'll be inside if you need me."

I hurried down the walkway to the back door. Only

when I closed the door behind me did I feel safe. I pressed my hands to my warm cheeks.

"Making a fool of yourself again, April," I chastised myself.

Chef appeared out of nowhere. "What have you done now, *ma cherie?*"

"It's not what I've done," I said, feeling a little woozy. "It's what's been done to me."

Chef raised his eyebrows. "Ah, I see." He leaned back against the counter, crossing one ankle over the other, the picture of elegant relaxation. "This is the moment I have feared for many months now."

"What are you talking about?" I asked.

"You are in love, *non?*"

"*Non!*" I spoke a little louder than necessary. "I mean, no. I don't believe in love at first sight. Do you?"

"Ah, *oui.*" He let out a wistful sigh. "I fell in love with my Marie the moment I lay eyes on her."

He had told me about the young woman who'd tutored him in French when he lived in Paris as a young man. "Was there ever another woman?"

He gazed into my eyes before turning away. "I thought I was in love with Norma, but it was merely... how do you say? Infatuation?"

When Norma had owned my home and ran her French restaurant, she used her beauty and elegance to manipulate men. One of the men under her thrall was Chef Emile Toussaint. People came from miles around to sample his creations, and Norma led him on to keep him working for her.

"But since then, I have learned that one can fall in

love gradually. Love can be more than a pretty face when one recognizes kindness, loyalty, and inner beauty in another."

"That kind of love is also for friends and family, not just lovers."

"Ah, yes," Chef said. "I mistook it for something else and felt sad that I could not be with…" He paused and looked away. "…with her. You have taught me that one can love another and not possess them."

There seemed to be a secret encoded message in Chef's words, but I didn't have a clue what it might be. I'd grown used to him being vague and mysterious.

"Have you ever thought that Marie might be out there somewhere waiting for you?"

His eyes became unfocused, as if he'd returned to his youth in Paris with Marie. She'd died at such a young age, and Chef had moved on but never forgot her. I hoped to inspire that kind of love someday, but I felt as if my chances might have passed me by.

Chef blinked, but one tear escaped. "She is in heaven, I am sure. An angel on earth, and now she is an angel above."

"You belong with her." I felt it in my soul.

"There is no room in heaven for the likes of me, I should think."

He began chopping vegetables and transferring them to a saucepan sizzling on the stove. I knew it wasn't real, at least not on the mortal plane, but I swore I could smell the aroma of onions and garlic.

I left him to his cooking and went to my favorite spot in front of the fireplace. I started a fire, and once the logs began to crackle and pop, I went back to the kitchen, but Chef was nowhere to be seen.

"You belong with Marie," I whispered.

I turned the kettle on to make a pot of my new wildflower blend tea. After it steeped for several minutes, I poured my first cup. As I inhaled the delicate floral aroma, I felt my shoulders relax for the first time that day.

I'd just gotten comfortable, enjoying the warmth of the fire, when the sound of pounding on my front door startled me. Irma pressed her face against the glass, then knocked again. I got up to let her in.

She started in on me the moment the door opened. "You didn't think to call me?" she railed. "You found a dead body and didn't bother to let me know? I thought we were a crime-solving duo, but I guess I was wrong. What's the deal? Did you get yourself a new sidekick?"

I did my best not to laugh, but my smirk must have given me away.

"You think this is funny?" she asked, putting her hands on her hips.

Her comment brought back the day's events and my urge to laugh evaporated. A man was dead—definitely not funny. Before I knew it, I was sobbing with tears running down my cheeks.

"Why am I crying when I didn't even know the man?" I asked Irma.

"Death can do that to a person, even a stranger's death." Irma led me back to the sofa. "Want some more tea?"

"And cookies?"

"Have a seat by the fire and I'll be right back." She picked up my cup and returned a minute later with another for herself and a plate of palmiers—little puff pastry cookies also known as elephant ears. She set the plate on the coffee table and plopped into a chair.

I'd wiped away the tears and blown my nose. "I hope the palmiers aren't stale. They're from the weekend, but I kept them in a sealed container."

"I'll take my chances." Irma took a big bite of her cookie. "Mmm..." she murmured as she chewed. "They're still good. Crisp and flaky." She finished two cookies before remembering why she'd come to see me. "So, tell me what happened to Quimby."

"Shot in the chest. I went to see him to find out if he was planning to use that ridiculous rumor about me and the sheriff to help get the sheriff recalled. When I got there, the door was unlocked but the place was empty. Turned out, Quimby *was* there. I found his body lying behind his desk."

"No way," Irma said before taking a bite of a third cookie. With her mouth full, she gestured for me to continue.

"Chief Deputy Rugger showed up and wanted to arrest me for murder."

Irma's mouth dropped open. "You? What the heck was he thinking?"

"He walked in on me and a dead body, so I don't really blame him. I had just found Quimby lying on the floor, and I didn't have a good reason for being there. When Freddie told hm that the time of death was well before I'd arrived, he gave up on that idea—not right away, but eventually. For a while there, I thought I might be spending the night in jail."

"Well, thank goodness Freddie managed to make him see sense." We sat in silence for a few minutes— Irma too busy eating cookies to ask more questions. "You say he got there shortly after you did? Did someone else report the murder first?"

I struggled to remember the chain of events. "I suppose someone might have heard the gunshot and reported it."

"Which was when?"

I closed my eyes, tired of questions. "I think Freddie said sometime between four-thirty and five." My eyes popped open again. "Oh. You're wondering how he got there so quickly. Do you think Rugger is involved in the campaign to recall Sheriff Fontana?"

"Maybe." Irma chomped on another cookie. "Or maybe he's the one who killed Quimby."

CHAPTER 8

There was something in the back of my mind I'd wanted to ask Irma. As I munched another palmier, it came to me.

"Do you know Krissyanne Dobbins?"

She nodded and washed down the last cookie with a few gulps of tea. "I don't know her personally. She's a volunteer, helping with the recall."

"A volunteer? Really?" I couldn't figure out why someone would work to unseat a popular sheriff when she wasn't even getting paid. "She looks like a soccer mom. At first, I thought she might be Quimby's wife, but I picture him married to someone more glamorous."

Irma raised one eyebrow. "You have no idea."

"What does that mean?"

"I'm sure you'll get a chance to see for yourself," Irma said.

When I couldn't coax more information out of her,

I gave up. I leaned back on the sofa and let the crackling fire lull me into a warm trance.

Irma brushed crumbs off her lap onto a napkin and stood. "I'd better get back to the cafe. I put Zoe to work in the kitchen and I need to make sure she's not distracting the other workers."

"The way you used to do?" From what Chef Emile had told me, Irma had been stunning at nineteen when she briefly worked for him. She distracted his sous-chef to the extent that he feared he might chop off a finger. Emile had convinced Norma to put Irma to work as a hostess instead.

"That was a very long time ago." Irma sighed as if a sudden wave of nostalgia had come over her. "Zoe's a very pretty girl, if you can look past the purple hair and black eyeliner."

"I have a feeling she wears that to annoy her mother more than anything else."

The back door opened and shut.

"Jennifer?" I called out.

"I'll be right there," she called back from the kitchen. "Is this a fresh pot of tea on the counter?"

"Yes, it's a new blend."

A minute or so later, Jennifer stepped through the door, holding a teacup. "Oh, hi, Irma. I didn't know you were here."

"Just leaving," Irma said, adding to me, "We'll talk more tomorrow."

After locking the front door behind Irma, I returned to my spot in front of the fire. Jennifer lifted her teacup to her lips. She inhaled deeply. "This smells heavenly. What is it?"

"I'm calling it my Spring Flowers blend. I started with a base of lightly roasted oolong and chamomile, then added rose petals, just a touch of lavender, and lemon balm for a citrus note. There's a little caffeine from the oolong, but not so much it should keep us awake."

"Too bad." Jennifer scowled. "I've got a test tomorrow and I need to study for it. A lot."

"Other than cramming for tests, how is school going?" I asked.

Her smile spread ear to ear. "I love it! There are so many history classes I can take. And art classes. If I want to transfer to a four-year university, I'll have to take certain courses like math and science, but I'll worry about that later."

"You're so young, and there's no need to rush into making a decision about what to do with the rest of your life," I said. "On the other hand, don't put off doing anything you really want to do, either. You'd be surprised how fast time goes by. You'll wake up one day and find yourself turning fifty and wondering where all the time went."

She gave me a knowing smile. "You've had a good life, April, haven't you?"

I smiled back. "The best part of my life has been when I showed up in town last year. I've never been happier." The events of earlier that evening rushed back into my mind. "If only dead bodies would stop turning up."

Jennifer gasped. "Dead bodies? Not again!"

I picked up our teacups and got to my feet. "I'll get us a refill and tell you all about it."

JENNIFER LEFT FOR SCHOOL THE NEXT MORNING BEFORE I came downstairs. I'd just sat down to a bowl of oatmeal with brown sugar, butter, and pecans when Irma walked through the back door.

"Don't get up." She leaned her walking stick against the counter. "I see there's been some progress with your not-so-secret garden."

"Slow progress." I tried not to make my disappointment obvious. "There's a fresh pot of coffee. Help yourself."

Irma got a mug from the cupboard and filled it to the brim.

"Where's Zoe?" I asked.

"I let her sleep in. She helped close last night. I have to admit, she's turned out to be a hard worker. I guess it runs in the family."

Setting her mug and her copy of the *Somerton Sentinel* down, Irma took a seat on the stool across from me. She had the paper delivered daily, even though she complained that it was run by a propaganda machine that cared more about catering to local businesses than reporting actual news.

She gestured to the paper. "You're on the front page."

I unfolded the paper, not looking forward to

reading it after the events of the day before. I groaned and read the sensational headline. "Murder in our Midst."

"Pretty thorough reporting for once."

Skimming the article, I slowed down when I spotted my name and read aloud, "A sheriff's department spokesperson identified April May, a new resident of nearby Serenity Cove, as the individual who found Ray Quimby's body. Chief Deputy Rugger arrived moments later and assessed the scene, quickly determining that Ms. May was not a suspect." I laid the paper down. "Quickly? Hah!"

"The article says Sheriff Fontana is going to handle the case personally," Irma said. "I wonder how that went over with Rugger, especially since he wants the sheriff's job."

"We don't know that for sure." I shrugged. "And for once, it's not my problem."

"Aren't you at least curious?" she asked.

"The sheriff will find the killer. I'm not a suspect, none of my friends are suspects, the murder didn't happen in my house—heck, it didn't even happen in town."

"But you're so good at solving murders." Irma crossed her arms and frowned. "And I'm a darned good sidekick. We'll get rusty if we don't get some practice in."

I laughed. "Okay, we can practice." I figured it couldn't hurt to humor her and discuss the case. "Who would you question first?"

She didn't have to think about her answer. "The

wife."

"Really? Not—"

"Wait," she interrupted. "Krissyanne. We need to find out if she was after Quimby's job, don't you think?"

"Yes, but she was babysitting when Quimby was shot." I got up and poured myself a second cup of coffee, adding a generous dose of creamer. "I wish I knew what incriminating information Quimby had on Sheriff Fontana. A rumor about another woman doesn't seem all that shocking, especially these days. And even if Quimby knew about the divorce, I don't think voters care that much, do you?"

"Divorce?"

"Oops." I'd forgotten that was supposed to be confidential. "Don't tell anyone I told you, okay? Cheryl's asked Fontana for a divorce, but she's agreed to wait until after the election."

I returned to eating my now-lukewarm oatmeal while Irma thought over what I'd told her.

"Some people were pretty unhappy that Cheryl got off with a slap on the hand for her involvement in the Maldonado murder," Irma said. "Fontana might go up in the polls if he announced his divorce."

"I hadn't thought of that, but you might be right."

Irma stood and grabbed her walking stick. "C'mon. Let's go question the sheriff first."

"Huh?" I didn't move from my stool. "We're not going to question anyone. Like I said, Sheriff Fontana can handle the investigation without our help. We're just practicing, remember?"

Irma crossed her arms and pouted. "Aw. You're no fun."

~

When Jennifer returned from class, she asked if she could invite Zoe over for pizza and a movie that evening. Zoe had been so exhausted from her first day of work that Irma gave her the night off.

Of course, I said yes and volunteered to provide snacks. Jennifer invited me to join them.

"Thanks, but I think I've watched *Pride and Prejudice* enough times," I teased.

She smacked me playfully on the arm. "That's not what we're watching. I'm going to let Zoe pick."

"You mean you'll let her pick which movie or miniseries version of *Pride and Prejudice* to watch?"

"Very funny." Jennifer skipped up the back staircase and left me alone in the kitchen.

"What snacks should I make for them?" I muttered to myself. A big bowl of buttered popcorn, of course, but maybe something more substantial to start off the evening. And something sweet to end it, of course.

"Flatbread pizzas!" I had a pack of flatbread in the freezer left over from a recent dinner. Add some toppings and I had a quick, relatively healthy savory treat.

"Pizza?" Chef's voice reached my ears before he shimmered into view. "I'm afraid I cannot help you there."

"You've already helped me." I retrieved the flatbreads from the freezer along with two containers of sauce. "You helped me make your *Sauce Tomat* which will be perfect as a base for the toppings."

Chef wrinkled his nose.

"I'm thinking some fresh mozzarella, tomatoes, and basil for one of the pizzas. And I might use pesto or alfredo sauce and add some marinated artichoke hearts. Oh—and caramelized onions. You taught me how to do that. If it weren't for you, we'd probably be eating canned soup and marshmallow crispy treats."

Footsteps on the stairs made me stop talking.

"Did I hear marshmallow crispy treats?" Jennifer beamed. "My mom used to make those all the time. She'd pretend she'd been slaving over the oven for hours, just like the commercial."

Darn. Now I'd have to make those. "I don't have the right cereal for it."

"No problem." Jennifer practically danced down the stairs and grabbed her keys from a hook by the back door. "Anything else you want from the store?"

By the time Zoe came over, I had enough snacks for a small movie theater. Good thing I liked leftovers, though young girls could eat quite a bit. Oh, to have their metabolism again, not to mention their energy.

They settled into the upstairs parlor, and I retrieved my laptop from the room as they discussed movie choices. My accountant had insisted that I send him all my financial reports, and I'd been procrastinating for too long. Running a tearoom wasn't as easy as I'd expected, but I didn't mind crunching a few numbers.

Tonight, I opened my laptop and struggled to focus

on the numbers. Considering I'd found a dead body the day before, it wasn't surprising that my mind was elsewhere. After an hour staring at the screen with very little progress, I decided movie night might be the distraction I needed.

Once I'd heated up another pizza, I carried it upstairs along with a pitcher of iced wildflower tea. It tasted surprisingly good cold.

Jennifer and Zoe sat on the sofa, their attention locked on the screen.

"Oh, *Little Women.*" I took a seat in the recliner and leaned back. "I haven't seen this version. Is that Katherine Hepburn?"

"Shhh…" came the reply from Jennifer.

"Fine," I grumbled, thinking she didn't need to be rude about it. "Oh, this is where…" I began but stopped when Jennifer shot me a glare.

Great. I'd joined them just at the saddest moment at one of the saddest movies ever made. Jennifer passed me the tissue box and I snatched a handful before passing it back.

Zoe must not have been familiar with the story, because she cried the most. She tried to hide it from us, but when the credits rolled, she blew her nose noisily. "Why did she have to die? It's so sad."

"I know." Jennifer sniffled. "I tried to warn you."

I wiped my eyes and left the two of them to discuss the plot and how they would rewrite the story so that no one had to die.

CHAPTER 9

*a*fter my morning shower, I stared into the mirror at my red eyes. Had I cried that much?

By the time I made it downstairs, I found a crowd in my kitchen. Irma, Zoe, and Freddie sat at the island while Jennifer worked the espresso machine. They greeted me with "good mornings," except for Irma who said, "It's about time you got up, sleepyhead."

"If I'd known there was a party downstairs, I would have gotten ready quicker." I glanced at Chef, who stood in the corner looking cross, no doubt unhappy about all the people disturbing his peace and quiet.

"*Zut!*" he exclaimed. "What are all these people doing in my kitchen?"

Unable to answer him in front of everyone, I leaned up against the counter and focused on my guests. No one spoke, which wasn't like them at all. "So, what brings you all here this fine morning? Did everyone wake up and find your cupboards empty, so you all decided to come here for breakfast?"

Irma held something behind her back. "We're not allowed to visit our friend?"

"What have you got there?" I reached for what I realized was a newspaper, but Irma passed it to Freddie.

"She's going to find out eventually, Irma." Freddie handed me the paper.

I unfolded it and read the headline. "Serenity Cove Resident Number One Suspect." My heart sank and I struggled to focus on the article. "Will someone give me the short version?"

Freddie spoke first. "It basically says you had no alibi and you had time to ditch the gun and wash up before returning to the campaign headquarters and pretending to find the body."

"Pretending?" I huffed. I had a feeling there was more to the story. "And?"

Four sets of eyes stared back at me until Irma finally filled in the rest. "And... it mentions that Quimby had dirt on the sheriff."

"Dirt involving you." Jennifer set a mocha latte on the island and Freddie guided me onto a stool.

"This is ridiculous," I muttered, scanning the rest of the article. Looking up, I asked, "Do people really think there was something going on between me and Sheriff Fontana?" When no one answered, I added more loudly, "Well, do they?"

Everyone mumbled, "No, of course not," and "Not at all," but I didn't buy it.

"You know how much people love rumors," Irma said. "It doesn't matter if they're true or not.

Gives them something to talk about besides the weather."

Jennifer raised her eyebrows. "Why? There are so many things you could talk about. Why resort to gossip?"

Zoe spoke for the first time since I'd come downstairs. "People don't want to talk about interesting things like history or books or axolotls."

"What's an axolotl?" I asked.

Zoe's grinned. "They're aquatic reptiles, and they're adorable! I wanted to get one for a pet, but my mom said no."

"Back to the subject at hand," Irma said. "How are we going to handle damage control and keep this from getting blown out of proportion?"

"Not much we can do," I said. "If I try to address the rumor, it will only make it worse."

"April has a point," Freddie said. "We need to ignore the rumors as much as possible until it blows over."

The doorbell rang and Jennifer hurried out of the room.

She returned moments later. "There's a sheriff's deputy here asking for you. I asked her to wait in the front room."

I groaned. "Now what?" I turned to the others. "Wait here. Hopefully this won't take long."

I immediately recognized the young woman in a sheriff's uniform who stood just inside the front door. Deputy Yolanda Lopez stood five foot four and lean, her hair in a get-down-to-business high bun. She greeted me with a slight smile and reached out her hand to shake mine.

She turned down my offer of tea or coffee, so I gestured to the sofa and chairs. We sat down in front of the unlit fireplace.

I got right to the point. "What brings you here, Deputy Lopez?"

"I'm assisting Chief Deputy Rugger on the Quimby case, and—"

"I thought Sheriff Fontana was investigating the murder," I interrupted.

"He was." She paused as if not sure how much information to share. "He's taken himself off the case due to some information that has come to light that might jeopardize the integrity of the investigation."

"Like what?" I had a feeling she meant the rumor about the sheriff and me, but I wanted to hear it from her.

The deputy ignored my question. "I'm here to get your statement." She took out a small notebook.

"Oh. I thought I'd have to come up to Somerton."

She smiled. "I don't get the chance to come down to Serenity Cove very often. You have a beautiful little town."

She asked me to repeat what I'd told her and Rugger on Tuesday at the recall headquarters. Was she looking for inconsistencies in my story? Or maybe she wanted to see if I'd change a crucial detail in my retelling. Telling the truth had its advantages. For one, I didn't have to try to keep my story straight.

"What's your relationship with Sheriff Fontana?" She asked the question without expression, though I bristled at the implications.

"I spoke with him a few times during his investigation of the Maldonado murder," I said. "But you already know that. You also know about rumors that small-minded people have been spreading because they're bored and don't want to talk about axolotls."

"Huh?"

"From what little interaction I've had with the sheriff, his actions and behavior have always been by the book. He doesn't tolerate dishonesty or cutting corners."

"You sound like a fan," she said, scribbling something in her notebook.

"As are most of the residents in this county, which is why I don't understand the recall campaign against him. It seems to me that someone has a grudge against him." I leaned back in my chair and crossed my arms. "How do you feel about your boss, Deputy Lopez?"

Her eyes shot to mine, surprised by my question. "Sheriff Fontana has opened up the department so that people like me could become deputies. It wasn't always like that. Ten years ago, they made it tough for women to get hired and even harder to make it through training. My aunt managed to become a deputy, but she quit after just a few months—the other deputies let her know she didn't belong. Sheriff Fontana cleaned up the department and got rid of the deputies who didn't…" She paused, looking for the right words. "…Who didn't belong in law enforcement."

I nodded. "He must have made enemies along the way."

"He did." The deputy set down her notepad. "Fontana teaches us to be loyal to the community and to the department rather than to be loyal to him or any other person. As a sworn officer, I need to be politically neutral, but just between the two of us, I think this recall is a joke."

"At least we agree on that much," I said. "What I don't understand is why the sheriff is off the case."

Lopez shrugged. "The victim was running the recall against Sheriff Fontana, so it's probably better he isn't involved in the investigation. I just have a few more questions and I'll get out of your hair." She picked up her notebook again and flipped a few pages.

"Has my alibi been confirmed by now so I'm no longer a person of interest?" I asked.

She waited a long moment before answering. "Not exactly. The city of Somerton recently began installing cameras on each road into town, but they're not all up and running as of yet. The highway from Serenity Cove to Somerton doesn't have any surveillance."

"Great," I said sarcastically. "Have you at least found the gun?"

Her mouth tightened into a thin line. "I doubt we ever will, but anything's possible."

"How far away was Quimby shot from?" The answer might determine whether the killer was an experienced shooter. I'd never shot a gun in my life.

"I can't give you that information."

"Is there anything you can tell me?" I asked.

She leaned forward. "I hoped there was something *you* could tell *me*. Do you have any insights into who might have killed Quimby or why?"

Had she heard that I'd helped solve murders in the past? I had planned to stay out of the investigation when I thought Sheriff Fontana would be in charge, but now, I wasn't sure. "The wife is always a suspect, of course and I'm sure you're looking into Krissyanne. As for why he was shot, Quimby had been digging up secrets. If he tried to blackmail the wrong person, that might have gotten him killed."

She nodded. "That's what I thought, too."

Not sure what she'd think if I suggested Chief Deputy Rigger might have killed Quimby, I kept those suspicions to myself. "So Quimby was blackmailing someone? Do you know who?"

"You don't want to know, trust me." She stood and I followed her to the door.

What the heck did that mean? "So, is this where you tell me not to leave town?" I asked.

She smiled. "Just let us know if you do."

The deputy got in her car and drove off, probably on her way back to sheriff's headquarters in Somerton. The peaceful view from my front door felt like a lie, with lazily crashing waves and clouds leisurely floating by. Peaceful moments in life were rare, which is why I treasured them.

Laughter came from the kitchen. What could they be laughing about at a time like this? Deputy Lopez's comments convinced me that Quimby had been blackmailing someone—maybe more than one person.

My determination to stay out of the investigation began to fade. Deputy Lopez was competent but inexperienced. I had no way of knowing if Chief Deputy Rugger would be biased in his investigation. Even the most honest person could be affected by their personal feelings, and I suspected Rugger wanted Sheriff Fontana's job.

When I pushed through the door into the kitchen, four heads turned in my direction.

"Can I talk to you in the other room?" I asked Freddie.

"Sure." She pushed her stool back and followed me back into the front room.

I led her to a table near the bay windows with their view of the ocean. "How far away was Quimby from his shooter?"

Freddie stayed standing. "April, I can't tell you details about a case that aren't public. Especially this case."

"Why this case?" I asked, but she didn't answer. She had given me information before, but I didn't bring that up. "Can you just tell me how good an aim someone would have to be to have shot him?"

She narrowed her eyes while I waited for her answer. "Chances are it wasn't the first time they'd shot a gun."

"That doesn't tell me much," I groused.

She crossed her arms over her chest. "Any other questions you want to ask me that I can't answer?"

I smirked. "Well, considering you can't tell me who all the registered gun owners are..."

"That is definitely not public information," Freddie said. "At least not in this state. But I can tell you there are a lot of concealed carry weapon permits issued in this county. Way more than the state average."

CHAPTER 10

$\mathcal{F}$reddie left to meet with patients. Irma and Zoe headed for home, and Jennifer went upstairs to take a quick nap, promising to come back downstairs to help get ready for opening.

After having the tearoom closed for three days, I felt behind. In a few weeks, crowds should begin to return to Serenity Cove, and I'd decide whether it made sense to stay open more hours.

I made a list of everything that needed to be done before we opened at noon. Leaving the cucumbers for Jennifer to slice, since it was one of her favorite tasks for some reason, I spread cream cheese on thinly sliced bread which helped to keep the cucumber sandwiches from getting soggy. Next, I mixed egg salad and sliced the ends off the Belgium endive to make smoked salmon endive boats. Those could be made a few hours in advance because there was no bread to worry about getting stale or soggy.

As I chopped and mixed, my mind swirled with

ideas of who might have killed Quimby. Every time a thought popped into my head, I wrote it down in a spiral notebook I left lying on the island.

Jennifer came down the back steps, rubbing her eyes and yawning.

"Wake up, sleepyhead," I said cheerfully.

"Just don't sing the Red Robin song, I beg of you." She made a beeline for the espresso machine and flipped on the power.

I laughed. "You're no fun." Apparently, I'd tormented her with the song one too many times. I hummed it to myself while she made her drink.

She carried her Americano to the island and began reading what I'd written. "'Find out who has experience shooting guns.' Do you think that's going to narrow it down much?"

"Well, sure. Only about 32% of Americans own guns." When she gave me a questioning look, I explained. "I looked it up online."

"I'm pretty sure it's higher in a small town like Somerton. Besides, you have Sheriff Fontana and Chief Deputy Rugger on the list as suspects. I bet they have great aim."

"They're only on the list for the sake of completeness. They've spent their entire lives upholding the law and putting bad guys in jail. Besides, I can't see either one of them risking their career and their pension. Although…" I paused, not sure how much information to share with Jennifer. "I'd love to know how and why Rugger got to the crime scene so quickly."

"Maybe Rugger was supposed to meet Quimby.

Maybe he found out something bad about Rugger. Or the sheriff."

"That's why I wrote this." I pointed to the notebook.

"'Find out what secrets Quimby had uncovered,'" Jennifer read aloud. "How do you plan to do that? We're not breaking into the campaign headquarters and hacking into his computer, are we?"

That didn't sound like such a terrible idea until I pondered it for a few moments. "I suppose that would be wrong."

"Wrong and illegal."

I handed her a cutting board, several cucumbers, and her favorite knife. "I guess we'll just have to do it the old-fashioned way—pretending to be a nosy neighbor and asking lots of questions."

"Do you think that will work?" Jennifer peeled the cucumbers, then cut them into thin slices as she talked. "No one is going to come out and tell you that Quimby had something on them. Especially if they murdered him for it."

I shrugged. "You can often learn as much from what people don't say as what they do. Not to mention body language."

Jennifer glanced at the clock and tilted her head to one side. "What's my body language telling you right now?"

I jumped off the stool and hurried to unlock the front door. It was time to open the tearoom.

The kitchen soon filled with the smell of scones baking in the oven. While Jennifer served afternoon tea in the front room, I arranged tiered tea trays and chatted with Chef Emile.

"Have you ever shot a gun?" I asked.

"*Ma cherie.*" He narrowed his eyes. "I was in the army during World War Two. What do you think?"

"Oh, that's right."

Jennifer pushed the door open. "Talking to yourself again, I see. Can you take an order on table eleven? I just seated three parties and I don't want to leave them waiting too long."

After taking the order and returning to the kitchen, Chef had disappeared, which disappointed me. I liked having someone to bounce ideas off of, even if he did get cranky with me.

I didn't see my friendly ghost for the rest of the afternoon. I hummed as I rolled out dough, doing my best to keep a steady supply of warm, flaky scones. They tasted best fresh out of the oven, especially slathered in clotted cream and jam or lemon curd.

After our last customer left, Jennifer loaded the dishwasher while I put all the leftovers away. The slow off-season meant we were able to do a lot of the cleanup as we went, so there wasn't much to do after we closed. I took off my apron and made a pot of Darjeeling tea, hoping the caffeine would revive me.

"Do you need anything in Somerton tomorrow?" I asked. "I thought I'd head over in the morning and pick up a few things at the grocery store. Our little store in town doesn't have much of a selection."

She gave me a suspicious look. "I don't suppose

you'll be stopping by the recall headquarters as long as you're there?"

I hesitated, not wanting to lie to her. She'd learned to read me like a book. "Okay, fine. I just want to see if Krissyanne is there. Just to ask a few questions."

"What if she's there alone? Are you going to question a potential murder suspect by yourself?" When I didn't answer, she said, "Fine. I'll go with you."

"You're going to protect me?" I asked, not trying to hide my doubt that my petite assistant would be any help in a crisis.

"Are you forgetting that I was state champion in my division in karate?"

I smiled. "I *had* forgotten. You're like a stealth weapon, small and cute on the outside, but deadly on the inside."

"That's right. And don't you forget it!"

EARLY THE FOLLOWING MORNING, JENNIFER AND I pulled up in front of the recall headquarters. I turned the car off but didn't get out.

"Thinking about the last time you were here?" Jennifer asked.

I glanced over at her. "Let's get this over with."

After putting money in the meter, I stepped through the headquarters' glass door with Jennifer close behind. A woman looked up from the same desk where I'd found Quimby. Her blonde-highlighted hair swept back from her face in stylish layers and her makeup had been applied impeccably. There was something familiar about her.

"What are you doing here?" the woman asked in an accusing tone, her eyes darting from me to Jennifer and back again.

"Krissyanne?" I marveled at the change she'd undergone since I'd seen her two days before.

She scowled. "Yes, what do you want? Returning to the scene of the crime?"

"You look really different, like you've had a makeover or something."

"I was very upset about Quimby," she said defensively. "I needed to cheer myself up, and I'd been meaning for ages to do something with my hair." She stopped speaking abruptly. "I don't have to explain myself to you."

"You look fantastic." I turned on the charm, hoping to disarm her. "I'm April May. I saw how distraught you were the other night. I hope you don't mind, but I wanted to check on you."

"Why?" Her eyes narrowed.

Pulling up a chair across from her, I took a seat while Jennifer stood behind me like my personal bodyguard. "Your colleague and friend died suddenly, and, well… I've found that people expect you to just get over something like that and get on with your life. But you have to come to this office every day. It must be so hard for you to sit at his desk and not think of what just happened."

"It's the only decent computer," she said.

I nodded knowingly. "No doubt. The volunteers always get the leftovers, don't they?"

"I worked for free," she said, the frown lines between her eyebrows deepening. "You'd think they could have at least gotten me a chair that didn't wobble."

I nodded sympathetically. "I hope they've finally recognized all your hard work and put you in charge."

Her shoulders slumped. "For now. We're supposed to have a meeting on Monday to discuss the organization going forward." Her eyes focused on her computer screen as if she had more important things to do than talk with me.

"I'm sure they'll see how dedicated you are. It must be hard to stay focused with the investigation and everything. Whoever's in charge has to see that."

She shot me a glance and smiled nervously, her expression quickly returning to neutral. "How am I supposed to get things done when Mr. Quimby's laptop is gone? I've been searching for our donor list for an hour, but he kept everything on his laptop like he didn't want me to see it." She frowned. "I bet the boss took it."

"Who is your boss?"

Her eyes shot to me. "Why do you want to know?"

"Oh, no reason," I said. "I thought I could put a good word in for you."

"Why?" she asked. "You don't even know me."

"No." I stood, figuring I wasn't likely to get much more out of her. "But I've been in that position before.

They'll probably bring in some outsider and ask you to train them." I shook my head. "It happens all the time."

She slumped even more, if that was possible, but said nothing.

"I'll let you get back to work." I had one more question before I left. "Who was the little girl who was with you when you came back to the office?"

"Oh, her mom's a friend of mine," she said, not taking her eyes off the monitor. "She needed her kid picked up from preschool, so I left work to go get her. Her mom was supposed to come by when she got off work, but that plan changed after what happened." She stopped and turned to me, a suspicious look in her eyes. "Why do you want to know about her?"

"Just curious. Cute kid." When I reached the doorway, I turned back and caught her watching me. We made eye contact briefly before she turned back to her computer.

Back in the car, I asked Jennifer if we could make one more stop.

She rubbed her hands together. "Who's our next suspect?"

I laughed. "You're enjoying this way too much. I thought we'd stop in to see Quimby's wife."

"Good choice. The spouse is always the number one suspect, right?"

"Right." I started the car and pulled away from the curb. "Just don't tell Irma you're my new sidekick. I'll never hear the end of it."

Ten minutes later, we pulled up in front of Superior Uniform Supply. The two-story brick building took up most of the block, with a parking lot full of delivery vans. I pulled into the lot and found a sign denoting visitor parking.

"Is this where the wife works?" Jennifer asked.

"I didn't expect such a big place." I hesitated, staring at the huge building. "I'm going to need an excuse to stop in to see Mrs. Quimby."

"We need uniforms for the tearoom?" Jennifer suggested.

"But why did we just show up and not call first?" I needed a better plan. "I mean we can say we just saw the building and stopped in, but how do we make sure we see Quimby's wife?"

Jennifer shrugged. "We either wing it or go on home. As long as we're here, we might as well go in."

"I suppose you're right." We exited the car and walked around to the front of the building, stepping through heavy glass doors into a homely lobby area. Photographs of the founder and current board of directors covered the walls, along with awards and commendations from a number of organizations, including a number of police and sheriff's departments.

I took a quick look at the management staff. Percy Jarman, CEO, had a round face and thick glasses. He looked too young to be running a big company, but maybe he was older than he looked. Or it was an old picture. I found a plaque from our sheriff's department from a decade earlier congratulating the uniform company for their excellent service from the former sheriff.

A clean-cut young man in a shirt and narrow tie entered the lobby. "May I help you?"

"I'm thinking about getting uniforms for my employees," I said. "Should I have called first?"

"No worries," he said with a wave of his hand. "Would you like a tour of our facilities?"

I glanced at Jennifer before saying, "Sure, why not?" I hoped it didn't take too long, since the tearoom would be opening in less than two hours.

He led us down a hallway past a row of offices. I glanced inside each one as we passed until a dark-haired woman in one of them screeched and jumped from her desk.

"You're April May," she called out for everyone to hear. "You killed my husband!"

CHAPTER 11

The woman hurried toward us as quickly as she could in her four-inch heels and tight skirt. Jennifer and I stood transfixed waiting to see what she would do.

She tossed her long, wild hair over her shoulder and grabbed my arm. "Come with me."

I didn't have a choice as she dragged me into her office. Jennifer hurried after me, managing to step inside just as the door slammed.

The woman put her hands on her hips. "Why'd you do it, April? Why'd you kill my sweet Ray?"

"I didn't kill him," I said, a whine slipping into my voice. I didn't like being accused of murder.

She pushed me into a chair and took her seat behind her desk. Jennifer hovered next to me with a stern expression, looking like she'd karate chop anyone who crossed her.

"He was a rascal and a scoundrel and a low-life loser, but he was my loser, and I loved him." The woman took a deep breath, expanding her ample bosom, then let out a dramatic sigh. "Tell me everything you know."

A quick glance at the plaque on the desk told me I was speaking with Ramona Quimby, Assistant Sales Manager.

"Well, Ramona," I began, "I found his body, as I'm sure you know. He'd been shot."

"Yeah, yeah. I know all that." She waved a hand dismissively. "What did Krissyanne do?"

"Krissyanne?" Her question caught me off guard. "She showed up a little later, after Chief Deputy Rugger. She'd just come back from picking up her friend's daughter. She seemed really distraught when she saw what had happened."

"Of course, she did." Ramona took an emery board from a drawer and began filing her nails. As if feeling us watching her, she said, "It keeps me from biting my nails when I get nervous or upset. How quick did the chief deputy get there?"

"Within minutes," I said. "He must have gotten a report from someone who'd heard the gun shot." I doubted my statement as soon as I'd said it. "Although that was at least a half hour earlier."

"Maybe Rugger was checking on something with my Ray."

"Like blackmail?" I asked.

Her eyes widened. "How do you know…" Her gaze drifted to Jennifer, then back to me. "You're just grasping at straws, aren't you? Testing the waters and seeing what pops up. Is that what you're doing here? Trying to shake a polecat out of a tree?"

I gave her a friendly smile. "I just want to get at the truth."

She studied her nails, then started filing again. "So you don't get arrested for murder?"

"Sure," I agreed. "It's not a pleasant experience. I assume you don't want to go to jail, either."

Her perfectly groomed eyebrows rose about an inch. "Me?"

"The wife is always at the top of the suspect list, as I'm sure you know."

She leaned forward, pointing her emery board at me. "I have an alibi. I was right here in a meeting until nearly six o'clock."

"That's good for you. Who were you meeting with?"

"I've told the police everything I know. I don't need to go through it all again." Her voice quivered. "It's been an awful experience."

"I want the person who killed your husband to go to jail," I said crossly. "Isn't that what you want? For someone to solve your husband's murder?"

"Sure, sure," she said, but she seemed to have moved on to other thoughts. "What kind of gun killed Ray?"

"I don't know," I said. "I don't think that information's been made public yet."

She leaned forward, her elbows on the desk and tapped the nail file in my direction. "That'd be the first piece of information I'd want if I were you. Now, me," she opened a drawer and pulled out a leather handbag.

"I like the Glock 19." She dumped the contents of the purse, and among a wallet, cosmetics, breath mints, and other items, a small, dark-gray gun slid onto the desk.

"I see," I said, my eyes as wide as saucers.

Ramona picked up the gun and thankfully pointed it at the wall instead of at me. "It's a 9mm luger—light, but not too light." She began shoving everything back into her purse, including the gun. "Plenty of people in town own guns, and lots of them have CCW's too, like me."

"CCW?" I asked.

"Carry concealed weapon permit," she explained. "I got mine when Ray was being threatened by one of his old business partners."

Jennifer tapped me on the shoulder and pointed to her wrist. I glanced at my phone, which said it was nearly ten-thirty.

"We've got to run." I jumped up and straightened my chair. "My tearoom opens at noon and it's a half-hour drive. Thanks for your time."

"Wait a sec." She retrieved a card from a holder on her desk and held it out to me. "Let me know if you want to grab a drink after work one day. Maybe we can compare notes."

I nodded and shoved the card into my pocket. "Sure thing. I'll be in touch."

A DRIZZLE BEGAN TO FALL AS WE REACHED HOME. WE found Irma waiting for us on the front porch when we pulled into the driveway. She wore a leather bomber jacket and a black beret.

She stomped her walking stick on the painted wooden flooring. "Where have you two been? You know you have a tearoom to run."

"We have an hour to finish prepping." I unlocked the front door, and Irma and Jennifer followed me, weaving through the flowered-tablecloth-covered tables to the kitchen.

Chef jumped when we entered and closed the book he'd been writing in. Was he hiding something from me?

I didn't have a chance to give it any more thought, because Irma repeated her question, more insistently this time.

"Where have you been all morning?" She leaned her walking stick against the counter and took off her jacket.

"How long were you waiting?"

She put her hands on her hips. "April May, if you're keeping something from me…"

"We stopped by to see Krissyanne," I said, feeling guilty somehow. "I just wanted to ask her a few questions about Quimby."

Her voice caught in her throat. "Without me?"

Not sure if she was about to yell or cry, I hurried to explain. "You're busy with your granddaughter. I didn't think you'd want to spend the morning driving to Somerton." When she didn't respond, I added, "I'm sorry I didn't call you first."

"Well, you should be."

I glanced at the clock. "We've got a lot to do before we open."

She took a seat at the island. "You can bring me up to speed while you work."

Jennifer made Irma a latte while I rolled out scones and told her about our meeting with Krissyanne. "She didn't want to tell me who's bankrolling the recall effort. I wonder why it's such a big secret. I have a nagging feeling it's connected somehow to Quimby's murder."

"It's an organization known as the Fair Practices for Safe Families Alliance," Irma said. "Talk about a bunch of gobbledygook. What does that even mean?"

"I need to know who's putting up the money to fund the recall," I said as cut out the scones and set them on the baking sheet. "Can you see what you can find online?"

"You know I'm no good at that stuff," Irma complained. She reached for my notebook, which was lying nearby, and flipped through the pages. "I see you've made a list of suspects. When are we going to go question Ramona Quimby?" When I hesitated, she scowled. "Well?"

"We stopped by Superior Uniform Supply after we met with Krissyanne and sort of ran into her."

Irma turned away and took a deep breath, doing her best to control her temper. "Darn. I wanted to get a chance at her. She's something, isn't she?"

"She sure is. She's invited me to go out for a drink one evening so we can talk. Too bad you're at the cafe every night."

"I can get away if I want to," she said. "I just don't want to very often."

A knock on the back door made me jump.

"Come in," I called out. When no one entered, I wiped my hands on a dish towel and went to open the door. "Oh, hi Zoe."

"Is Irma here?" she asked tentatively.

"Sure is. Come in out of the wet."

She wiped her feet on the mat, then stepped inside and took her coat off. Before I could close the door, Whisk sauntered in, weaving his way between our legs. His leopard-spotted fur glistened with moisture from the misty drizzle outside. Since I still held the dish-towel, I wrapped it around him and gently dried him off.

Whisk made little mewing noises that sounded like a cross between gratitude and complaining. When I removed the towel, he gave me a trill and jumped down to the floor. Instead of escaping up the stairs to his attic hideaway, he hurried over to Zoe and began rubbing against her legs.

"Hello there." She reached down and picked him up before I could tell her he didn't like strangers. To my surprise, he snuggled up into the crook of her arm, appearing perfectly content.

Irma gave me a puzzled look. "He never lets *me* pick him up."

"He barely tolerates me." I watched Zoe as she talked sweet nothings to my barely tamed cat. Her face softened as she stroked his fur, and I couldn't help but think Whisk somehow knew that Zoe needed a friend.

"He really shouldn't be in the kitchen while I bake." Luckily Whisk had stayed in the attic when the health department had made their inspection. "Would you mind taking him upstairs?"

"Can I stay with him a little longer?" Zoe asked.

"It's okay with me if it's okay with your grand-mother, but I've got work to do." The tearoom would be opening in a few minutes, and I still had scones to bake.

Zoe turned to Irma. "Can I, Grandma?"

"I'll come back and get you in an hour or two." Irma carried her cup to the sink and put her jacket on. "Are we meeting with Ramona tonight?"

"I want to talk to Freddie first and see what infor-mation she's willing to share. Have you noticed she's not nearly as forthcoming as she was last year?"

"We had an incompetent police chief back then, remember?" Irma reminded me. "Freddie had to go around him to accomplish anything."

"Not just incompetent. Crooked, too."

"True. Since Sheriff Fontana took office, he cleaned up the department and got rid of the bad apples."

"All of them?" I asked.

She narrowed her eyes. "Is there something you're not telling me?"

"I just had a thought." I put the first batch of scones into the oven. "If the sheriff is recalled, Chief Deputy Rugger will take his place, won't he?"

"I suppose so," Irma said, sounding hesitant. "At least until there's another election. What are you suggesting?"

"I think we should go talk to Rugger tomorrow morning. Might as well see if we can talk to Sheriff Fontana while we're at it, though I guess you'll have to go without me. He doesn't want to be seen with me."

"Oh, right," Irma said, picking put her walking stick. "Tomorrow's Saturday, you know."

"Darn. I wonder if Rugger works weekends. It might have to wait until Monday."

AFTER A QUIET FRIDAY IN THE TEAROOM, JENNIFER AND I didn't have much to clean up. We had lots of food prepped for the weekend, so I told Jennifer she could call it a day.

"Yay!" She clapped her hands. "Zoe and I are going to karaoke night at the hotel."

"Karaoke?" I repeated. "There really isn't much to do in Serenity Cove, is there?"

Jennifer shrugged. "It's fun. You should try it sometime."

I ignored the suggestion. "That's really nice of you to spend time with her since she doesn't know anyone in town."

Jennifer tucked her phone in her pocket and pulled out her keys. "I'm not doing it to be nice. There's hardly anyone my age in this town, especially during the off-season. And I still haven't made any friends at school. I like having someone to hang out with."

And I had no doubt that Irma liked her granddaughter hanging out with Jennifer. Few young women were as mature and sensible as my assistant.

As soon as she left, I pulled out my phone and dialed Freddie.

When she answered, I asked, "Do you have plans for this evening?"

"No…" Freddie's voice sounded tentative and maybe a little suspicious. "But I'm wiped out from my week, between seeing patients and my coroner duties."

"What if I bring dinner over to your place? I've got a freezer full of food. You can choose between jambalaya and beef bourguignon."

I could almost hear her smile through the phone. "Beef bourguignon sounds wonderful. I'll supply the wine." She paused. "Are you going to pump me for information?"

"Not until at least dessert." I knew that was her weakness. "I've got chocolate cheesecake mousse. Sugar free and keto friendly, whatever that means. It's your favorite."

"Give me half an hour to straighten up a bit," Freddie said. "But I'm not promising you any information that's not public, no matter how good your food is."

"Turn your oven on to 350 in about fifteen minutes and I'll warm up dinner at your place."

I defrosted the freezer bag with two servings of beef and poured it into a casserole dish. After retrieving three servings of chocolate cheesecake mousse in case Freddie wanted seconds, I packed everything into my car.

Nearly forgetting a fresh loaf of crusty French bread to go along with our meal, I came back inside and picked up my notebook. I paged to my preliminary list of suspects and stared at the sheriff's name.

Sheriff Fontana's life was in turmoil. His wife planned to leave him, and a recall campaign had been initiated to remove him from his job. Almost anyone could be pushed to the breaking point, and I wondered how far Quimby had pushed Fontana with his slander and rumor mongering.

Had Quimby gone too far? Everyone had their breaking point. I wondered what it would take to make the sheriff snap.

CHAPTER 12

I drove to Freddie's house just a few minutes away. Just like everything in Serenity Cove. Her little cottage welcomed me with a bright porch light and a warm glow coming from behind the windows. I carried my heavy tote bag full of food up the brick walkway. The door swung open just as I reached the top porch step.

Freddie grabbed the bag, and I instructed her to set the timer for thirty minutes. Once the food was warming in the oven, with dessert safely in the refrigerator, Freddie handed me a glass of white wine.

"Thanks." I took the glass and settled on the sofa. "I know technically I should be drinking red wine with beef, but I like white better."

"I've got red too if you decide to switch."

Having been warned not to ask questions until after dinner, I did my best to stay on neutral ground. "Busy week?"

She titled her head. "Yes, a murder tends to add to my workload."

"That's not what I meant, but I suppose that's why you said you were beat. Your practice is quiet this time of year, isn't it? Without all the tourists?"

She took a sip of her wine and relaxed back into her chair. "I do my best to motivate my patients to schedule routine needs during the off season, but an awful lot of people won't call me until there's a health crisis. Our town's population is aging, and I worry about them. We're a long way from the nearest hospital."

We made more small talk until our dinner was ready, then moved to the dining table to eat. Freddie poured me more wine, though I held up my hand so she'd stop at half a glass.

"Your beef bourguignon is delicious," Freddie said with a contented sigh. "And I'm glad you brought French bread so I can sop up every last drop."

"You mean Chef Emile's beef bourguignon," I said with a chuckle. "He doesn't like when I take credit for his recipes."

"But you do all the work," she said. "It hardly seems fair."

I leaned back in my chair unable to eat another bite. "He might think it's not fair that I'm alive, and he... isn't."

"You sound sad," she said, pushing her plate away. "April, have you fallen in love with your ghost chef?"

I nearly spit out the sip of wine I'd just taken. "No, of course not. Don't be ridiculous." I stood, ready to take our plates to the kitchen, just steps away. "I've gotten used to having Chef Emile around, that's all."

"Go get comfortable in the living room and I'll do a quick clean up and start a pot of decaf."

Once I returned to the sofa, I took out my notebook and flipped to my list of suspects. Freddie returned and offered me more wine, but I turned her down since I had to drive home. She took a seat across from me.

"Tell me," she began. "Why are you getting involved in this case? You're no longer a suspect, after all."

"I hope you're right, but I'm not convinced I'm in the clear. Rugger's got it out for me, and I don't want to wait for him to decide to arrest me."

"I see…" Freddie didn't sound convinced.

"I've come up with some possible suspects." I held out my notebook, showing her my list. "I met Ramona yesterday. She's… interesting."

She raised one eyebrow. "That's one way to put it."

"She carries a 9mm gun. In her purse. At work. Who carries a gun around in their purse?"

"You'd be surprised," Freddie said. "Most people don't advertise that they're carrying. As long as she's got a CCW permit, it's perfectly legal. And since I know you're going to ask, no, Quimby wasn't shot with a 9mm. But that doesn't tell us much. I wouldn't expect someone to hold onto a gun after killing someone."

"Good point. Notice who else is on the list?" I asked. When she didn't answer, I spelled it out for her. "Sheriff Fontana and Chief Deputy Rugger."

Now both eyebrows went higher. "You think one of them killed Quimby?"

"I don't know, but it's possible. Quimby dug up a lot of dirt on Fontana. Maybe Quimby uncovered a secret that the sheriff didn't want to be exposed."

"And Rugger?"

"Rugger showed up within seconds of me calling 9-1-1. He could have shot Quimby, then cleaned up and returned, watching the office to see if someone showed up. Then he bursts in so he can take control of the situation and direct the investigation in a certain direction." I let that sink in for a moment. "If not for you, he would have arrested me completely throwing suspicion away from himself."

"That's not a terrible theory," Freddie admitted. "Though I hate to think it might be true."

"I don't want to think it either. I'd hoped that Sheriff Fontana had removed all the bad elements from his department. I want to believe they're all above reproach, but if they're not…"

Freddie nodded slowly, beginning to understand my dilemma. "So, you're getting involved because you're not a hundred percent sure about the integrity of the investigation by the sheriff's department?"

"Exactly. It might be a case of the fox investigating the murder at the hen house."

~

As I turned left onto Ocean View Drive, blue and red lights flashed in my rear-view mirror. I pulled over and rolled down my window.

Deputy Alex Molina appeared next to my door. He spoke. "License and registration, ma'am."

"Hello, deputy," I said. "I'm going to reach into my purse for my driver's license, and my registration is in the glove compartment."

Molina lowered his voice. "I wanted to talk with you, Ms. May." He took the driver's license I handed him and pretended to study it. "I heard you found another body."

"It's not my fault." I heard defensiveness creep into my voice. "I stopped by to talk to Quimby because I'd heard he'd been spreading rumors about me. I don't like people spreading gossip, especially when I'm the subject."

"I believe it was a rumor involving you and the sheriff." He handed back my license. Raising his voice, he asked for my registration again.

I fumbled through the contents of my glove box until I came across the registration which I handed him.

"There's nothing between the sheriff and me," I said firmly. "Nothing."

"I know that," Molina said. "Someone wants to get rid of the sheriff, and they're willing to go to great lengths to do it. The recall campaign wasn't going anywhere, in spite of what Quimby said—the sheriff is too popular. I'm worried whoever's behind it is going to use the murder to take down the sheriff."

"How are they going to do that? Lots of bad press if he doesn't solve it?"

"Possibly," he said. "Or maybe worse."

"Worse?"

"I can't say any more than that." He handed me back my registration. "Be careful. If you get involved, as I know you probably already are, there's a good chance you'll be putting yourself in danger. Someone has murdered once. They'll do it again if they think someone is getting in the way. I don't want that someone to be you."

Goosebumps ran up my arms. "You're serious."

"Deadly serious."

CHAPTER 13

*S*aturday morning dawned gray and gloomy. I shuffled downstairs and found my assistant as sunny as ever. She took one look at me rubbing my eyes and quickly got to work making my cappuccino.

Setting it in front of me, she said, "You used to love this misty, drizzly weather."

"I love this weather in small doses, but when it's day after day after day…" I took a careful sip of my hot drink and sighed. "Thanks. This is just what I needed."

Irma burst through the back door, dripping water everywhere. "Your not-so-secret garden is turning into a mud pit," she announced, flinging her raincoat over a shelf in the storeroom. Pulling off her muddy boots, she joined us in the kitchen in her stocking feet. "I'm starting to think the sun's never going to come out again."

"My sentiment exactly," I grumbled.

"Cheer up," Irma said. "We've got suspects to question and a murder to solve."

"Those are waking me up." I pointed at her bright orange- and purple-striped socks. "Are you the wicked witch of the east or the west?"

"Very funny." Irma took a seat next to me.

"Why don't you text the sheriff and see if he or Rugger are available to meet this weekend? He doesn't want any evidence of us communicating until all this blows over."

Irma pulled out her phone and I gave her the sheriff's cell phone number. She typed her text on her phone while Jennifer started making her a mocha latte. They both finished about the same time.

Irma scowled at her phone. "I hate texting. I'm all thumbs. And I never understand all the shortcuts, like smh and tbh. Are people really in that much of a hurry that they can't spell things out?"

"Smh?" I asked.

"Shaking my head, according to Zoe. That is one of the benefits of having a teenager in the house. I think she's going to help keep me young." She stared at the phone. "No answer yet."

"We've got lots of reservations this weekend for some reason," I said. "Looks like Jen and I are going to be busy. I sure hope they don't all cancel when they see the weather."

Irma stood. "I'm going to go home and wake up Zoe. If I don't, she'll sleep until noon."

"But you've barely touched your mocha." Jennifer grabbed a to-go cup from the cupboard and poured the drink into it.

Irma took it from her. "You're a good kid. Don't let anyone tell you different."

I followed her to the back door and let her hold onto my arm while she put her boots on. As she headed down the walk and rounded the corner of the house, I stared out at the piles of rocks. Irma was right. The recently turned earth had become a giant mud puddle. As a child, I would have been thrilled and hurried to put on my raincoat and boots to go play and make mud pies. But now, all I saw was a mess that would take weeks to dry out. My dreams of a summer unveiling of my new garden feature were fading quickly.

~

LUCKILY, NEARLY ALL THE GUESTS WHO'D RESERVED tables that weekend showed up. With a roaring fire in the fireplace, and plenty of hot soups and stews, not to mention freshly baked warm scones, everyone seemed to enjoy having afternoon tea while stormy skies threatened outdoors.

We hadn't been this busy since summer. As I helped Jennifer carry plates and trays back to the kitchen, I told her so.

I began loading the dishwasher. "Do you think it's because there's so little to do when it's rainy?"

She thought for a moment. "That might be it. Also, afternoon tea is such a cozy thing to do, don't you think? Especially on a cold, wet day like today."

I considered her theory. "Maybe I need to start

marketing our tearoom as a cold-or-wet event. 'Cold, gloomy weather getting you down? Come to Serenity Tearoom where the scones are always warm and toasty.'"

Jennifer scrunched up her face. "Scones are toasty?"

"Fine. If you don't like my slogan, you can see if you can come up with a better one."

⁓

IRMA DIDN'T HEAR FROM THE SHERIFF UNTIL SUNDAY evening. He agreed to meet us the next morning in an out-of-the way location.

Since Sheriff Fontana didn't want to be seen with me in public, I dressed in baggy jeans and T-shirt along with brown hiking boots. Irma brought over a wig for me to wear, along with an oversized navy-blue windbreaker.

We took separate cars to Hiverton. Irma drove her 1985 Cadillac El Dorado at exactly five miles over the speed limit, and I followed at a reasonable distance until we reached the edge of town. Suddenly, Irma's car made a sharp right turn, tires squealing.

My heart beat faster as I followed her around the corner. Was she in danger? Another turn, this time a sharp left, but when I followed her onto the street—no sign of the Cadillac. I slowed down at each cross street and looked both ways but didn't spot the car.

"Crazy old lady," I mumbled, hoping her erratic behavior didn't mean anything more sinister. I had the address of the diner where we were meeting Fontana, so I headed in that direction.

The Black Crow Diner stood on the main street, and I wondered why Irma had made her crazy turns. If I didn't know better, I'd think she was trying to lose me. But if that was the case, she'd failed, since I spotted her car the moment I turned into the parking lot.

I pulled into a spot at the far end of the parking lot and watched as Irma got out of her car and walked to the front door. I texted her: *What was all that about?* but she didn't respond.

As planned, I waited five minutes before entering. I did my best to change my posture, hunching over as I lumbered into the diner. It seemed like overkill to me, but I'd started to enjoy the feeling of working under-cover, except for the itchy wig.

Fontana and Irma sat at the booth to my left, so I nodded to the server approaching me and headed toward them, taking a seat at the next booth with my back to Fontana. I put my arms on the table—big mistake. I dug in my purse for a pack of wipes, and cleaned off the table, but the stickiness remained.

After we'd ordered and I had a cup of coffee and an enormous blueberry muffin in front of me, I heard Fontana tell Irma, "Who's she supposed to be? Mata Hari?"

"The fifties' flapper wig was the only one that would fit her big head," Irma said.

Big head? Wait until we got home. At least I didn't need a booster seat, like my tiny friend.

"Why did you want to meet me?" Fontana asked once he was sure no one was near enough to eavesdrop. "I'm guessing it was April's idea."

"And mine," Irma said. "I'm her sidekick."

"Sidekick?" Fontana said, doubt in his voice. He began chuckling.

"It's not funny," Irma said. "Someone is dead, and we're not sure your department is doing everything it should to find the murderer."

"What does that mean?" A note of defensiveness crept into his voice.

I decided to jump into the conversation. I lifted my phone to my ear so I appeared to be on a call. I spoke just loud enough for Fontana to hear me. "Do you know who hired Quimby? You know, the person behind your recall campaign?"

"No," he responded softly. "I haven't been able to find out."

While I ate my muffin, Irma took over questioning the sheriff. "Do you think your chief deputy might be the one who got this recall petition started?"

"Rugger?" Fontana obviously hadn't expected that question. "Why would he...?"

"So he could have your job," Irma said. "Obviously."

After a long silence, Fontana spoke again. "I suppose it's possible."

The server, a plump woman who'd probably worked there since it opened, brought over a pot of coffee to my booth. "Want a top off?"

"Sure." I pushed my coffee cup so she could reach it.

Next, she checked on the sheriff and Irma before going back behind the counter.

"Was Quimby blackmailing you?" Irma asked, blunt and direct as always.

Fontana sighed loudly enough for me to hear. "He tried. He said he could hush up the rumor about me and April. For a price. I told him to do his worst. I have nothing to hide."

I washed down the last of the muffin with a few gulps of strong coffee. "Does Rugger have something to hide?" I whispered.

The silence that followed my question led me to wonder if Fontana was even breathing. Irma and I waited for his response while I pretended to stare out the window. In reality, I was watching them in the reflection of the window.

Irma wasn't as patient as me. "Well?" she prompted, waving her fork at him.

"I don't know." His shoulders slumped. "He's a good cop. I'm sure of it. But just about everyone has secrets —things they'd rather the general public not know about."

I pretended to talk into the phone again. "You know he showed up at the murder scene right after I found the body. Do you know what he was doing there?"

"He said the call went out and he answered it. Said he was just a few blocks away when he heard it."

"A few feet away is more like it. It couldn't have been more than a minute or two—I was still on the phone with the 9-1-1 operator when he arrived. And he didn't seem all that surprised to find Quimby dead if you ask me."

"I'll have to look into that," he said, his voice empty of emotion. "Anything else I should know?"

"Ramona Quimby has a gun, but apparently so do half the people in this county."

"You're probably not far off."

CHAPTER 14

As soon as I'd driven a block away from the diner, I pulled off the hot, itchy wig and ruffled out my hair. I couldn't wait to get home and change into my normal clothes.

Irma pulled up next to me at a stoplight and motioned for me to roll down my window. "Wanna stop by and see if Krissyanne is at the recall head-quarters?"

I frowned. "I'm afraid she'll think I'm harassing her if I visit again so soon. I just went and talked to her on Friday, and she really didn't tell me much." My desire to get home and change fought with my drive to get more information. "I sure would like to find out who's behind the recall campaign, though."

"Too bad you didn't bring some of your shortbread cookies to butter her up with," Irma mused.

"Um..." I reached into my purse and held up a baggie full of cookies I'd packed that morning. "I always bring cookies with me. You know, in case of emergency."

"Right." Irma didn't seem to buy my story. "Follow me."

I followed her boat of a car several blocks until she turned into a strip mall parking lot. She parked in front of a greeting card shop and got out.

"What are we doing here?" I asked as I followed Irma inside.

She went to the gift bag section, found a bright pink bag and some tissue paper. "Here. Pay for these and we'll be good to go."

We left Irma's car there, and I drove us to the recall headquarters just a few blocks away. On the way, Irma put the cookies in the gift bag.

Once she'd fluffed up the tissue paper, I said, "You have skills I never expected."

"You have no idea." Her impish grin stopped me from asking what she meant.

We parked a few doors down from the recall head-quarters and fed the meter. When we stepped through the door, Krissyanne looked up from her desk with a suspicious glare. Did that woman trust anyone?

"We were in the neighborhood," I said, introducing Irma. "I brought you some of my famous shortbread cookies. I don't know if you make it out to Serenity Cove very often."

She took the bag of cookies and peeked inside.

"They're not poison," Irma said. When Krissyanne's eyes widened, she added, "In case you were wondering."

I smacked Irma on the arm. "Quit saying that to people."

"I'd like to sign the recall petition," Irma said. "I think the sheriff needs to be removed from his position. Can I volunteer to get more signatures? If you get me a clipboard and some of those petitions, I bet I can get a bunch from my neighbors."

I kept quiet, impressed by Irma's improvisation skills.

"Oh, yes. Right." Krissyanne stood and began searching through drawers. "I'm not sure where they keep the petitions. Ray was always so secretive, hiding things from me." She picked up a cardboard box off the floor, set it on her desk, and began rummaging through the contents.

"Really?" Irma asked. "Like what kinds of things? Secrets?"

Krissyanne stopped and gave Irma a withering stare. "I thought you wanted to sign the petition."

"I do. Maybe you can call whoever's in charge." Irma plopped down in a chair. "I'll wait."

Krissyanne bit her lip and looked from Irma to me and back again. "I don't think Mr. Jarman—" She stopped herself from finishing her sentence. "I mean, why don't you come back tomorrow. I'm sure I'll have everything organized by then."

Irma appeared to think it over. "I suppose I could do that. Although with the price of gas these days…" She stood and headed for the door. "C'mon, April. I have a restaurant to run."

With a quick goodbye, I followed Irma out the door.

"Great work," I said, impressed that she'd gotten a name out of Krissyanne. "Now we just have to find out who Mr. Jarman is. It's not exactly an unusual name." A memory niggled at my brain. "Although it sounds familiar for some reason."

"I have confidence that you'll figure it out."

"Wait." I threw out my arm to stop her just as we reached my car. "Pierce Jarman is the CEO of Superior Uniform Supply."

"Okay. So?"

"He's Ramona Quimby's boss. I bet she got her husband a job with the recall committee."

"You might be on to something," Irma said as she opened the car door. "But more importantly, did you give all the cookies away? I'm starving."

~

After stopping at Irma's favorite Somerton bakery for more cookies, I dropped her back at her car. I followed her taillights all the way back to Serenity Cove until she turned on her street. By the time I pulled into my driveway, the sun began peeking out behind fluffy white clouds. I hoped our gray, drizzly days were over, at least for the time being.

Hoping to get a peek at my secret garden, I pulled all the way forward in the driveway. Not expecting to see much progress after all the rain, I gasped at the sight of six-foot tall stone walls spanning the back of the yard.

George emerged from the side door of the garage

carrying a metal gate. My heart soared. It was the most beautiful gate I'd ever seen, with an aged patina, scroll-work, and other details. I'd seen a picture of it and given my approval, but the real thing was even more special, with antique charm and elegance. The perfect gate for my secret garden.

"Do you need help with that?" Looking around for Levi, I asked, "Where's your helper today?"

"Are you saying I'm too old for this job? Because if you have any doubts about my capabilities, I can give you a prorated refund. I've got plenty of other people who want to hire me."

"I just thought…" I began. Changing the subject, I attempted to get back on his good side. "That's a stunning gate."

George grunted in response, and I decided to let him get on with his work. I entered the kitchen and found Chef rolling out dough that only he and I could see.

He looked up. "Have you returned from your sweetheart?"

"What are you talking about?" I asked.

The kitchen door swung open, and Jennifer appeared. "You've gone from talking to yourself to having arguments with yourself." She shook her head. "If I didn't know any better…"

"I'm not losing my mind," I snapped.

"Sorry…" Her smile faded. "I didn't mean anything like that. In fact, I've been meaning to tell you—"

"No, I'm sorry. I think this case is getting to me. I didn't mean to be short with you." I turned and ran up the back stairs to the second floor. When I reached the attic door, I opened it and made my way to the top of the steps. "Whisk?" I called out.

At least there was one creature in the house who would listen to me without judgement. Sometimes you needed someone you could just vent to, without lots of questions or suggestions.

"Whisk?" I called again. I walked the outer edges of the attic, being careful to step on rafters. I'd planned to have flooring installed for safety, but then my former handyman had left town. I had no idea if he was ever coming back.

I'd once thought I'd felt something for Mark, but it turned out to be only physical attraction. We had little in common. More importantly, he couldn't handle it when he found out I saw ghosts.

Would I ever have a man in my life who would accept my abilities? It took me quite a while to accept it myself.

Whisk was nowhere to be found, no doubt on one of his excursions. I worried about him running loose around the neighborhood. Cars went too fast on the side streets, and I'd heard that coyotes sometimes came into town from the nearby hills. But Whisk refused to be trapped inside the house. I'd tried once and spent a night listening to him howl and screech followed by neighbors' complaints the next morning.

As I gathered my thoughts, I couldn't shake the guilt over how I'd spoken to Jennifer. Her good nature always allowed me my outbursts of temper, but I needed to do a better job of controlling myself.

I made my way to the window and called out one more time, "Whisk? Are you out there?"

From up here, I could see the entire coastline past the hotel to the cliffs that isolated us from the rest of the towns up and down the coast. In a way, I'd isolated myself in Serenity Cove, in this tiny town of 964 residents.

Tucked away in my tearoom, so much had managed to reach me despite living in such a secluded location. Murder and greed, but also friendship, family, and contentment.

Was I contented? My contentment was only surface level—I felt something missing. A soulmate? A partner? Someone to hold me when I was sad or celebrate with me during life's happiest moments.

As I made my way back down two flights of stairs to the kitchen, I told myself I didn't need anyone else. I had everything I needed right here.

But did I?

CHAPTER 15

*R*est of Monday

The kitchen was empty, and I hoped that Jennifer hadn't escaped to her room to avoid me. I'd transferred a roaster chicken from the freezer to the refrigerator to thaw and needed to cook it soon. My supply of stock had diminished over the cooler months, so making another batch seemed like a good project for the day.

Chef didn't correct me nearly as much as usual. Either I'd become a better cook, or he'd decided he'd never make a true chef out of me. When he scolded me for having the burner on too high, I caught myself before I snapped back at him. Instead, I bit my tongue and thanked him for mentioning it.

Later in the afternoon, Jennifer came down to tell me she and a friend were going to TacoTaco for dinner. Before I got a chance to tell her I'd decided to turn over a new leaf and not snap at people, especially her, a horn honked.

"That's them." Jennifer hurried out the front door.

Chef watched me as I worked, and I wondered if he knew what I was thinking.

"She doesn't seem to be mad at me," I began to strain the broth through a colander into a large bowl.

"Why would she be mad? You pay her for her work, do you not?

I set aside the chicken and vegetables, then ran the stock through a fine-mesh sieve. The last step, straining the broth through cheesecloth, took the most patience, especially since Chef insisted I strain it several times.

After taking a break to root around in the refrigerator, I lunched on leftover quiche, then returned to the stock.

"Emile?" I called out softly. When he didn't answer, I went ahead and poured half the stock into a silicon container and put it in the freezer. The other half went into the refrigerator. Tomorrow, I'd decide what soup to make.

I felt drained, not sure if it was all the time spent in the kitchen or the unsolved murder that I couldn't stop thinking about. After a warm cup of chamomile tea, I climbed the stairs to my room.

A SUNBEAM SHONE THROUGH MY WINDOW, AND I blinked awake, throwing the comforter aside and hurrying to the window. I peered out the window, disappointed to see thick, dark clouds gather and hide the sun from view. Heavy raindrops began to fall like giant's tears.

Shaking off my resentment at the weather, I tried to remember my delicious dream. The more I tried, the more it slipped away.

I gave myself a quick pep talk. "Today's going to be a good day." After all, I once loved rainy days before they hurt my business. And since I decided to stay closed on Tuesdays during the off season, I didn't have to worry whether we'd have any visitors to the tearoom. And we'd be closed tomorrow, too. I could do anything I wanted. Or at least anything indoors.

I hummed a tune as I showered and took my time getting ready. A little mascara never hurt anyone, I told myself. I spritzed my wrists with my favorite floral cologne, then danced down the stairs, determined to keep a positive mood.

Four glum faces greeted me when I entered the kitchen—Jennifer, Irma, Zoe, and Freddie. My heart sank into my stomach.

"What's wrong?" I asked. "Is everyone okay?"

Irma handed me the morning paper. "Sheriff Fontana has been arrested for murder."

"Everything went down last night," Freddie said as I took a seat at the island. "I only found out this morning. Not sure how the paper got the story in time to print it in the morning edition."

"How?" I began. "Why?" My brain wouldn't form the complete question.

"I'll make you a double cappuccino." Jennifer flipped on the espresso machine.

Zoe joined her. "Can I help?" I guessed she didn't feel comfortable discussing murder, and I didn't blame her.

Freddie explained. "There was an anonymous tip, as I understand it, and Rugger got a search warrant for the sheriff's home. They found Quimby's missing laptop—"

"That doesn't mean he killed Quimby," I interrupted, wondering why the sheriff would have the laptop in his home.

Freddie placed a hand on my arm. "They also found the murder weapon."

I blinked, not believing what I heard. "That's not possible. Why would the sheriff shoot Quimby? Just to keep from being recalled? The recall effort probably wouldn't have even succeeded, but even then, is that really worth killing for?"

"You're right," Freddie said. "That's not worth killing for."

Steeling myself for more bad news, I waited to hear the rest. "But there's more?"

"E-mails from the sheriff soliciting bribes might give him a motive."

"No way." I waved my hand, almost knocking over the cappuccino Jennifer held out. "Sheriff Fontana was as honest as the day is long. Longer, actually."

Freddie shrugged. "You can't argue with evidence."

I jumped off my stool, now wide awake. "You can if it's been faked. Sheriff Fontana isn't an idiot. If he had shot Quimby, he would have gotten rid of the gun. And if he'd taken the laptop, he'd have destroyed it. He knows how to delete files so they'd never see the light of day. He's being framed."

"Now, April," Irma said. "I know you like the sheriff, but—"

"This has nothing to do with how I feel about Fontana," I said. "It's common sense." Taking in each face staring at me, I asked, "Am I alone on this?"

Freddie answered first. "Honestly, it seemed fishy to me the moment I heard about it."

"Me too," Irma said. "It stinks more than rotten fish. And I should know, considering my restaurant is right next to the pier."

I chose not to ask her to elaborate. "What are we going to do?"

"What we do best," Irma said. "We're going to solve a murder."

"Again," Jennifer added.

Zoe's confused gaze wandered from Jennifer to Irma. "You're going to do what?"

"Just remember," Irma said. "I'm the number one sidekick."

ZOE SQUEALED AS A CRACK OF LIGHTNING LIT UP THE house.

Jennifer began to count, "One thousand—" when a

crash of thunder shook the house. Even Freddie jumped.

"The fence next door is on fire!" Jennifer jumped off her stool and grabbed the fire extinguisher from the wall.

"Hand it to me." I'd had to put out a trash fire recently, so I took it from her and ran out into the pouring rain. I doubted the fire would persist in the downpour, but better to be safe than sorry, as I'd always been told.

The rain fell nearly sideways, and I fought the wind to get to the fence where I sprayed the smoldering wood. "That should do it," I muttered and hurried back inside.

Jennifer waited just inside the door with a towel which she wrapped around me. "You're soaked! Go upstairs and change."

"Yes, ma'am." I chuckled at her motherly tone. "By the way, I'm really sorry about snapping at you yesterday. I don't know why you put up with my outbursts."

"April. You're in the middle of a murder investigation. You've been accused of murder. I'd think something was wrong with you if you didn't have an occasional outburst."

Forgetting how wet I was, I gave her a hug. "Sorry. Now you're wet too." I hurried upstairs to put on dry clothes.

Once I'd changed and towel dried my hair, I returned to the kitchen. The four women had vastly different expressions. Freddie checked her watch, possibly confirming how long she had until her first patient of the day. Jennifer flitted around the kitchen, making sure everyone had enough to eat and drink. Zoe's eyes darted around the room, not sure what to make of the situation.

And as for Irma, she twisted a napkin in her hands and stared out the window at the rain, her face contorted in worry.

"You can stay here until it calms down," I said, assuming she was worried about getting home in the downpour. My words didn't appear to calm her. "I wouldn't want to go out in this weather either."

Without a word, she left the kitchen and went into the tearoom. I followed her to the front windows where we watched the churning sea across the street. A huge wave rose from the sea, and I gasped as it crashed across the road, a river of water lapping my front lawn.

"Maybe we're not as safe here as I thought." The water receded, but I stiffened, waiting for the next onslaught. "Still, I suppose this old house has survived other storms in the past hundred plus years."

Irma didn't respond. She turned her gaze south toward her restaurant. The Mermaid Cafe was too far away even on a clear day to see from my home, but Irma seemed oblivious to that fact. At that moment, I knew the source of her anxiety—her restaurant.

"Your restaurant must have survived plenty of storms over the years." I hoped my words were encouraging but doubted it.

"Barely," she said, barely above a whisper. "If this gets any worse—"

An even bigger wave crashed over the road, the

water coming all the way up to the porch. Heavy rain fell sideways as the wind rattled the windows. We both jumped as a huge branch fell from a neighbor's tree, landing on the sidewalk.

I touched Irma's shoulder. "Why don't we go back in the kitchen?"

She glanced at me before turning back to the window. "You go. I'd like to stay here." She must have sensed my hesitation. "I want to be alone for a bit."

Up until a few days ago, I'd been the closest thing Irma had to family. But she had a granddaughter now, and I figured it was time to test that relationship. I had a feeling Zoe would pass with flying colors.

I pushed the kitchen door open and addressed Zoe. "I think your grandma needs you."

Zoe's eyes widened. "My grandma?" She gave a nod of understanding and left the room.

Jennifer handed me a freshly made cappuccino. "Is Irma okay?"

I took a seat at the island. "There have been worse storms than this, right?"

Freddie grimaced. "This storm isn't over yet." She took a deep breath and let it out. "The last really big storm was in 1983 I think, before I was born. But old timers still talk about the storm of '66, not long before the Mermaid Cafe was built. It washed the pier away."

"Ugh. But surely they wouldn't build a restaurant next to the pier that couldn't withstand a similar storm."

"I'm sure that's what Irma is hoping too."

~

THE STORM SHOWED NO SIGN OF WINDING DOWN. THE sound of the rain pelting the house only got louder.

Chef paced one end of the kitchen. I'd never seen him look so nervous.

He stopped and turned to me. "Difficult memories are returning to my mind. In 1959, I believe it was, the sounds of the storm kept us up all night. We placed sandbags around the house, but the water still seeped in."

I nodded to encourage him to continue.

Jennifer noticed my nod and nudged me. "What are you staring at?"

"What? Nothing." I considered Chef's statement. "Do you think we should put sandbags around the house?"

"Do we have sandbags?" Jennifer asked.

"No. After this storm is over, I'm going to make sure we're better prepared for future storms."

"Smart thinking." Jennifer stared out the window. "The storms seem to get worse every year."

I tapped Irma on the shoulder. "Okay, sidekick. Time for us to get to work." What better distraction from the storm than a murder investigation?

Freddie stood, looking hesitant to leave. "I'll call the clinic and see if they can reschedule my appointments for today. I don't think it's safe to drive right now." She stepped into the front room to make her call.

"What can Zoe and I do?" Jennifer asked.

"We don't need to involve Zoe," I said. "I don't think

her mother would like it if she found out we got her mixed up in a murder investigation."

Zoe piped up. "But I want to help."

"That's my girl," Irma said proudly, adding to me, "But nothing dangerous, okay?"

How could she help while staying safe? "Well… Jennifer's really good at research." I knew Jennifer could find historical information in a flash, but we didn't need that skill at the moment. "Maybe the two of you could find us some information online?"

She snapped to attention. "What do you need us to find out?"

"Whatever you can about Pierce Jarman, CEO of Superior Uniform Company. We're looking to see if he has any ties to the recall campaign or anything hinting that he might have a grudge against the sheriff." I tore a sheet of paper out of my notebook and started writing. "First, find out if his company still has the contract for the sheriff department's uniforms. Second, any organizations or affiliations, he has, political or otherwise. Third…" I wracked my brain to think of what other information might be helpful.

Jennifer snatched the paper from me. "We'll find out everything we can and report back to you."

I grinned. "You're the best."

"What can the two of us do in this weather?" Irma waved her hand toward the rain pelting against the window. "We're not going out in that are we?"

"Hopefully the cell phone towers don't get knocked down. There's one person in law enforcement who has an open mind and might give us some information." I set my phone on the island and dialed, placing it on speaker mode.

A recorded voice came on the line. "Serenity Cove Police Department. If this is a life-threatening emergency, call 9-1-1. Please listen carefully as our menu options have changed."

I disconnected the call. "Do you happen to have Deputy Molina's cell phone number?"

"Deputy Molina?" Irma asked. "Why do you want to talk to him?"

"He's the one person I know is on our side."

CHAPTER 16

When I finally got through to Deputy Molina, he scolded me for bothering him.

"Did you not notice that there's a major storm surge?"

"I thought you'd be all cozy at your desk," I explained. "Surely, no one is committing any crimes in this weather."

He snorted. "My job entails public safety, not just arresting criminals."

"I just had a few questions," I began, but the phone had gone dead. "He just hung up on me!"

Irma shrugged. "Or the phones went down." She pulled her phone out of her pocket. "I still have two bars, but he might be on a different carrier."

"I'll try calling back." I hit send, but it went straight to voicemail.

Irma stood and walked to the window, frowning at

the pounding rain. "I guess we'll have to see what we can accomplish without him."

"And without leaving the house. This storm is not making it easy for us."

"Okay, so who else can we call?" Irma asked.

"I wouldn't mind having a few words with the Chief Deputy." I picked up my phone again and looked up the sheriff headquarters' number. A woman answered, telling me Rugger was in a meeting and couldn't be disturbed.

"I'd like to make an appointment to meet with him," I told the woman.

"And what is it regarding?" she asked.

After a moment's indecision, I decided on the truth. "The Quimby case. I have some information I think he would find pertinent."

"Deputy Yolanda Lopez is handling that case," she said. "I'll put you through."

Before I could stop her, she'd transferred me to Lopez, who answered on the second ring.

"Hello, Deputy," I said. "It's April May. I was wondering…"

"Hold on," she whispered. I listened as footsteps, undoubtedly hers, tapped on a hard floor. A door slammed and she spoke again in a hushed voice. An echo made me wonder if she'd gone into a closet. "April. I'm so glad you called. Where are you right now?"

"I'm at home," I ignored Irma's facial expressions indicating she wanted to know what was going on.

"I'll meet you there," she said. "Give me an hour. I want to make sure no one sees me."

"I don't think you should go out in this storm." I stared at the phone. "She hung up. Don't people say goodbye anymore before they hang up?"

Irma scowled with impatience. "Fill me in."

"Deputy Lopez is on the case," I explained. "And here I thought for sure Rugger would handle it himself."

"Makes sense." Irma returned to her stool at the island. "This way he can appear to be uninvolved, though I'm sure he's the one really running the show."

"No doubt," I agreed. "Lopez is meeting us here in about an hour. We should know more then." I stared out the window at the raging storm. "Assuming her car doesn't float away into the ocean."

IRMA AND I SAT AT ONE OF THE TEAROOM TABLES BY THE front window. We drank nearly an entire pot of tea while we watched and waited for Deputy Yolanda Lopez to arrive.

A late model gray sedan pulled up across the street and a woman got out wearing a baseball cap and a rain poncho.

"That must be her." I pointed her out to Irma. "I'm not sure if she meant to be in disguise, but I would hardly recognize her in her rain gear."

Lopez leaned into the wind, holding the hood of the poncho low to shield her face from the pelting rain.

When she walked away from the house, I began to wonder if I'd mistaken someone else for her. Then she crossed the street and headed our way. The poncho whipped around her body in the gale-force winds. She might be trying to appear as if she were out for a stroll, except that no sensible person would be out in this weather.

I lost sight of her. "Where'd she go?"

A knock on the back door answered that question. I hurried through the kitchen and let her in. She stepped inside, pulling off her wet poncho, which I hung on a hook by the door. She stepped into the kitchen, her keen eye taking in every detail.

"Irma and I are having tea in the front room." I gestured for her to follow me.

"I'd rather stay in here, if you don't mind," she said. "Just you and me."

I grimaced. "Irma's not going to like that idea."

The moment I said those words, the door swung open, and Irma appeared. "Are we meeting in here?" She seemed to sense the deputy's hesitance, because she added, "It's okay. I'm April's sidekick."

Deputy Lopez looked from me to Irma and back to me, one corner of her mouth twitching. "What the heck. I'm probably committing career suicide as it is. Why not have one more witness to my downfall?"

"Have a seat, deputy." I motioned to one of the stools around the kitchen island. "You look like you could use a nice cup of tea and some homemade short-bread cookies."

That got a weak smile from her. "Call me Yolanda,

please." Under her breath she added, "I probably won't be a deputy for much longer anyway."

I bustled about making tea while Irma set out cups and plates. Irma also got out the cookies, since she'd learned all my secret spots where I tried to hide them from her.

Once we were all seated with our tea and cookies, I waited to see what Yolanda had to say before peppering her with my questions. Irma waited as well, showing uncharacteristic patience.

She stared into her teacup, and I wondered if she trusted us. If not, why had she come, especially in this weather?

Finally, she spoke. "I think Sheriff Fontana is being framed."

"Of course, he is," I said.

"We already know that," Irma added.

Yolanda chuckled. "Molina was right. You're on top of things." Her shoulders relaxed and she took a sip of tea.

Irma held out the plate full of shortbread cookies to her. "Then why'd you arrest him?"

The deputy accepted a cookie and took a bite. "We got an anonymous tip. The caller—"

"A man or a woman?" Irma interrupted.

"I listened to a recording of the call," Yolanda said. "It could have been either. I think they were deliberately trying to disguise their voice without making it too obvious. If I had to guess, I'd say it was a woman making her voice sound lower than normal."

"Please go on." I gave Irma a pointed look intended

to stop any more interruptions. "What did the caller say?"

"That they'd seen Sheriff Fontana leaving the recall offices at around the time of the murder carrying a laptop. Rugger told me to get a search warrant, so I did. I didn't expect to find anything..." Her voice trailed off.

"But you did," I said. "Not only the laptop, but a gun. I'm assuming ballistics confirmed it was the murder weapon."

She nodded. "Not only do I believe the sheriff is innocent, but it defies logic. No one in law enforcement would harbor evidence in their own home. The laptop I suppose I could understand, if he wanted to see what was on it or if he wanted to make sure he permanently deleted all the files, but he could have easily wiped it clean in less than an hour. Or, he could have cloned all the files and thrown it in a dumpster."

"My thoughts exactly." I refilled our cups while waiting to see what else Yolanda had to say.

At that moment, what sounded like a herd of elephants came running down the back stairs from the second floor. I turned to see Jennifer and Zoe with big grins on their faces. Jennifer stopped in her tracks when she saw Yolanda, and Zoe ran into Jennifer, almost knocking her over.

"I'd better go." The deputy stood and headed for the back door.

"Wait, Deputy," I said as she reached for her poncho. "I have a feeling you're going to want to hear this."

She hesitated, but after a moment, she returned to

the kitchen. She stayed standing as if ready to make a quick getaway.

"What did you learn about Pierce Jarman?" I asked the two young women, adding to Yolanda, "In case you didn't know, he's the CEO of Superior Uniform Supply and Ramona Quimby's boss."

Jennifer spoke first, her words escaping in a rush. "Superior Uniform used to be the supplier for the county sheriff's office. It was a multi-million-dollar contract that got renewed for the past ten or twelve years or so."

"Until Sheriff Fontana came on board," Zoe said, unable to contain her excitement. "The sheriff asked for an audit, which turned up some… um…"

"Irregularities," Jennifer said, completing her sentence. "We found some old tweets accusing Jarman of bribing Fontana so he'd renew the contract."

Yolanda, who'd been listening carefully, spoke up. "I could have told him that there's no way Fontana would take a bribe."

"He claimed it was a campaign contribution," Jennifer said.

"So, what happened?" I asked.

"The sheriff put out an RFQ—that's a request for quote—to several other uniform suppliers and disqualified Superior Uniform," Jennifer said. "And that's when the feud began."

"Tell them about the party," Zoe said.

"Jarman has this huge house up in the hills just outside Somerton," Jennifer said.

"Like huge," Zoe added. "You should see the pictures."

"He had this big fundraiser for a PAC," Jennifer went on. "That's a political action committee. They had celebrities and everything. It was like ten thousand dollars a person."

"This is all very interesting," Yolanda said, "but what, if anything, does this have to do with Quimby's murder?"

"We think Jarman was behind the recall campaign, and now we know where he got the money," I said. "Ramona Quimby got her husband connected with Jarman. She probably told him her husband would do anything for a buck."

"That's believable based on his record." Yolanda shut her mouth tightly and mumbled under her breath, "You didn't hear that from me."

"As far as I'm concerned, you were never here," I said with a wink. "Anyway, I figure part of Quimby's job was looking for dirt on the sheriff."

"Okay," Yolanda said. "But I still don't see how that helps us find the murderer."

"What if Quimby realized that he wasn't going to find any dirt on the sheriff," I said. "But he found dirt on someone else—someone with deep pockets. Someone like Jarman."

"Hmm…" Yolanda took a few moments to consider my ideas. "Not a bad theory."

"And then Jarman decided to get rid of Quimby. And then—"

Yolanda held up a hand to stop me. "But I could

come up with probably a hundred other theories that are just as plausible. Without any evidence, theories don't do anyone a bit of good."

I felt myself deflate like a punctured beach ball. Did I have anything more than theories? "Okay, then let's talk evidence. Besides the gun and laptop that were obviously planted at Fontana's house, what other evidence do we have?"

"I can't tell you anything that hasn't been released to the public yet."

"Like the letter written in blood?" I asked. "Remember, I was the first one there after Quimby was shot. It looked like an 'R' to me. R for Ramona?"

"Maybe," she said. "Or it could have been a 'B' or even a 'P.' For all we know, it doesn't mean a thing."

Jennifer nudged Zoe. "I told you they needed our help. Let's go back upstairs and see if we can find some real evidence." The two of them clomped back up the stairs.

When Yolanda, Irma, and I were alone again, I pulled out my phone. I found the picture I'd taken of the email the night of the murder and showed it to Yolanda.

"Who gave you this?" she asked suspiciously.

"No one. I took it at the recall office shortly before I found Quimby's body. It was lying on top of the desk." Just lying there waiting for someone to find it. "What kind of person would shoot someone, take their laptop, and leave an incriminating email out in the open?"

"It might have had nothing to do with the murder," she suggested.

"You don't really think that, do you? I thought cops didn't believe in coincidences."

"Coincidences do occur, you know," she said. "I'm guessing you think it was planted." When I nodded, she agreed. "I thought so, too. We didn't find any fingerprints on it. Well, except yours."

"I didn't know there'd been a murder when I picked it up or I wouldn't have touched anything."

Yolanda drew her eyebrows together. "I wish you hadn't touched anything."

"Why do you say that?"

"Rugger says we arrested the right person, but he's got a backup suspect just in case the sheriff turns out to be innocent."

"Let me guess," I said glumly. "Me."

CHAPTER 17

*Y*olanda pulled her still-wet poncho over her head and slipped out the back door. The wind had died down, but the rain still fell steadily.

I wiped up the floor with a towel and threw it into the hamper before returning to Irma in the kitchen.

"It's time." She stood with a solemn look on her face.

"Time?"

"To see what's left of the Mermaid Cafe." She slipped into her raincoat, pulling the hood over her head. She hurried to the front door as if I was going to let her go by herself.

"Hold on." I grabbed my jacket from the closet. "Did you walk here?"

She pointed to her Cadillac El Dorado in the driveway. "Luckily it didn't float away."

"That car? My car could have used your car as an anchor."

Irma was too tense to react to my attempt at humor. She'd reached her car before I stepped onto the front porch. I pulled open the passenger door and climbed in.

The car crept along the street, the shore on our right, until we reached the pier minutes later. Or rather what was left of the pier. My heart leapt when I saw the front of the Mermaid Cafe intact.

"It survived!" I blurted out, immediately regretting my words. As we pulled into the parking lot next to Irma's restaurant, I could see that the front wall was all that remained standing. The rest of the place had been reduced to rubble.

Irma stopped the car and got out. Not sure what to do, I stayed in the car to give her a few moments to herself to let the truth sink in. The restaurant had been her life ever since she'd given up her baby and returned to Serenity Cove fifty-five years earlier. She'd sunk all her money, time, and energy into making it a place where locals and tourists would feel welcome.

As I watched her survey the damage, I wondered what she would do now. Would she rebuild? Most people her age would have retired years ago, but I couldn't imagine Irma spending all her time at home in front of the TV.

I got out of the car and walked over to where she stood, staring at the cliff where her restaurant had stood for decades. She seemed oblivious to the rain as she gaped at what remained of her restaurant.

We stood side by side, watching the waves crash against the rocky shore. A sunbeam broke through and was quickly swallowed up by dark clouds. The storm wasn't over yet, but it would be soon. The sky would clear, and volunteers would clean up the debris from the beaches and streets and within days, some residents would forget there'd ever been a storm. But Irma's life would never be the same.

After several minutes of silence, Irma nudged me. "Let's go."

"Okay." I followed her back to her car. "You're welcome to come back to my place for as long as you want."

She said nothing until she pulled into my driveway. "I think I need to be alone."

"What about Zoe?"

She clutched the steering wheel so tightly her knuckles were white. "I just… I can't."

"Can't what?" My compassion for her loss mingled with frustration. "You are so used to being on your own, Irma Vargas, that you don't know what it means to let someone in. If you don't let that girl into your life —into the good stuff and the hard stuff—you're going to regret it."

Irma blinked, fighting back tears. I'd never seen Irma cry, and I would bet the last tears she'd shed were when she gave up her baby, Zoe's mom.

"Wait right here," I ordered. "I'll send her out."

I crossed my fingers that Irma would listen to me for a change and hurried inside. I found Jennifer and Zoe in the kitchen.

"Your grandma needs you," I said to Zoe. "Hurry up before she leaves."

"She's leaving?" Zoe asked.

I held her by her arms. "Irma needs you. She doesn't know it, but she does. And I'm pretty sure you need her just as much. I don't want either of you to let your pride or your independence get in the way. Go. Now."

Zoe hesitated for just a moment, then ran from the kitchen and out the front door.

THE NEXT MORNING DAWNED CLEAR AND BRIGHT. As I came downstairs, the view out my front windows looked picture postcard perfect except for the fallen tree branches strewn along the street.

I joined Jennifer in the kitchen.

"Have you heard from Irma?" She flipped the switches on the espresso machine, and it began to hum and whir.

Before I could answer, the back door flung open. Irma burst into the room, with Zoe right behind. She didn't appear as distraught as I would have expected, but Irma often hid her feelings.

"What a gorgeous day." Irma gave me a broad smile and set her walking stick against the counter. "Don't you agree, April?"

I glanced at Zoe who raised her eyebrows as if to say I was on my own.

"Yes, it's a lovely day," I said. "And you're in an unexpectedly good mood, considering."

"Life's too short. I've been tied down to that restaurant for decades. It's about time I made a change. Zoe and I are going to travel."

Zoe's mouth dropped open. "We are?"

"You like to travel, don't you?" Irma asked. "Or we could move to... I don't know, Istanbul? New Zealand?" When she didn't get a reaction, she added, "Paris? Well, we don't have to make up our minds right now."

"Why don't you sit down and have a muffin," Jennifer suggested. "I'll make you and Zoe cafe mochas unless you'd like something else."

"That reminds me," Irma said. "We still have a murder to solve."

I stopped with my muffin halfway to my mouth. "Muffins remind you of murder?"

"With all my newfound free time, maybe I could be a full-time sidekick. I wonder if there's any money in it."

I chuckled. "I wouldn't know. Maybe you could volunteer for the sheriff's department."

"Maybe, but they might have too many rules for a rebel like me. Anyway, before I make any decisions about the future, we need to find out who really killed Quimby."

I was impatient to get to the truth, too. "I did want to try and see Molina today. I'm hoping he'll be willing to share some information with us."

"Sounds good," Irma said, her voice muffled by the huge bite of muffin she'd just stuffed into her mouth. After she chewed and swallowed, she said, "Maybe I'll become a private detective. Or go to work for one. What do you think?"

Jennifer set a mocha in front of Irma. "That sounds... interesting."

Irma's overly positive mood disturbed me, considering she'd just lost the restaurant she'd poured her heart and soul into for more than five decades. Was this the denial stage of grief?

"There's lots of things you could do," I said. "There's no rush to decide on anything."

"I'm not getting any younger, you know."

"None of us are," I reminded her, though she had a good head start on the rest of us. "Now finish up your drink and let's go."

We took Irma's Cadillac to our local police station, hoping that would lessen the chance of me being spotted. Irma offered me her flapper wig again, but just the thought of it made me itch. I tucked my hair up into a wool cap instead.

Walking down the empty hall toward Molina's office, my heart began to pound as I remembered his warning that the murderer might kill again. We needed to clear the sheriff's name, while making sure that no one else ended up dead.

How did I, a former software programmer and current tearoom owner, end up involved in solving murders? I'd had no idea when I moved to Serenity Cove that it was anything other than the sleepy little coastal town it appeared to be.

I pushed open the door to the police station and we

walked past the empty reception desk where Pauline used to sit. I asked Irma if she'd gotten another job.

"I heard she went on a cruise," Irma said.

I knocked on Molina's door hoping he was in. We really needed his help if we were going to clear the sheriff's name.

"Come in," he called out, and we entered his small office. "Oh, it's you."

"Nice to see you, too, Deputy." I took a seat across from his desk and Irma sat next to me.

Molina leaned back in his chair. "I hope you're beginning to see what's at stake. This isn't a fun little puzzle for you and your friends to figure out."

I ignored his comment. "You've met Irma Vargas, haven't you?"

"Ma'am." He nodded in her direction. "Sorry to hear about the Mermaid Cafe. You must be devastated."

"I'll get over it," Irma replied curtly. "Your department arrested Sheriff Fontana for a crime he didn't commit."

"I think you know he didn't kill Quimby," I added. "So, if you expect me to sit around while he's railroaded, you don't know who you're dealing with."

"Of course, he didn't kill Quimby," he said.

His statement took me aback. "Then why are you sitting here instead of trying to get Fontana out of jail? When is his bail hearing?"

"This afternoon," he said. "It's likely that they'll refuse bail based on the circumstances."

"Circumstances?" Irma leaned forward in her chair. "We have to do something. He doesn't belong in jail."

"Jail is probably the safest place for him right now," Molina said. "Did you ever think of that? They'll keep him separate from the other inmates, of course. And with him as the prime suspect, everyone else is safer, too. The murderer will relax and let his guard down, and you know what that means."

I nodded. "I hope it means they'll be easier to catch."

"Exactly. If we're lucky, they'll make a mistake, and I'll be waiting when they do."

"You've learned a lot since I first met you, Deputy. But it's not safe for you to go digging around behind your boss's back. I assume Rugger is in charge of the investigation for the time being?"

"Deputy Lopez is officially in charge. But Rugger is supervising, of course."

"Do you trust him?"

Molina stared at the wall and didn't answer right away. When he finally spoke, I saw doubt in his eyes. "I want to trust him. I've never been given a reason not to. Until now, that is. But I'm not sure he's seeing things clearly. If Fontana goes to jail, Rugger will take over as sheriff, I have no doubt about that. And as interim sheriff, he'll most likely get the job officially at the next election."

"I can see how Rugger has a possible conflict of interest, but what I'm wondering is whether he also has a motive."

Molina's eyes jerked wide. "For murder?"

"If Quimby had something on Rugger, killing him could take care of two birds with one stone—keep Quimby quiet and take over as sheriff. Rugger showed up at the recall headquarters way too quickly. It allowed him to take control of the situation."

Molina scowled, deep in thought. "No way. I want to clear the sheriff just as much as you do, probably more. But if that's the direction you're headed, don't come to me for help."

I stood. "If you're not going to keep an open mind, then you're no help to me, and you're certainly no help to Sheriff Fontana."

Irma got a few words in herself. "We're going to find out who the killer is. I don't care if it's the sheriff, Rugger, or my best friend April May." She jabbed an elbow in my direction. "Let the chips fall where they may."

Irma turned and stormed out of the room. I gave the deputy a nod and hurried after her all the way to the parking lot. She didn't slow down until she reached her car.

"Nice job," I said. "A little dramatic, but effective."

"We'll see." She glanced back at the building as if wondering what effect she'd had on Molina. "Where next?"

"I'll send Ramona a text and see if she wants to grab drinks after work," I said. "And I'd love to talk to Krissyanne again and see what she knows about the laptop." I stopped and pictured the office the day I'd found Quimby's body. "I don't remember a laptop at the recall headquarters on the day of the murder. Whoever killed him must have taken the laptop, then planted it at the sheriff's house."

"With the gun."

"Exactly."

"We should go back to the recall headquarters." Irma asked. "To talk to Krissyanne."

I frowned. "I think we've outworn our welcome with her. Unless we come up with an excuse to visit, I think it's best if we back off from her for at least a day or two."

Irma nodded in agreement. "The grieving widow it is then."

CHAPTER 18

We arrived at Blondie's Bar and Grille about ten minutes late thanks to Irma's insistence on changing her outfit five times. She ended up wearing a chic, hot-pink pantsuit, matching pink sunglasses, and a fedora. I'd chosen my outfit with the intention of blending in—jeans and a knit top.

Stepping through the door, Irma followed me into the cocktail lounge. A long bar ran along one side of the room, with a number of high-tops taking up the rest of the space. I stopped to take a look around, and Irma ran into me.

"Take off those sunglasses," I hissed. I swore I could feel her glare at me though I couldn't see her eyes.

"But they make the outfit," she protested.

"Take them off."

She reluctantly removed them and tucked them in her pocket. "Do you see Ramona?"

"I do." I headed for the far corner where I'd spotted the former Mrs. Quimby. She wore a short black skirt, white collared shirt and high heels, looking every bit the high-fashion version of a modern professional woman. As I approached her, I wondered how much of Ramona Quimby was an act and how much was real.

"Oh, hey," she said in greeting. "Pull up a chair."

I introduced Irma and we ordered drinks—a white wine for me and a Purple Haze cocktail for Irma. Ramona pointed to her empty glass and told the server to bring her another.

"I like to check out the specialty cocktails at other restaurants when I get the chance," Irma said after ordering. "Do you have to be blonde to work here at Blondies?" she asked the server when she returned with our drinks.

"Yeah, but you can wear a wig if you want. Want to order any food?"

I glanced at Ramona, who shook her head. "Maybe later."

"Happy hour ends at six," the server said before moving on to another table.

"Cheers." Ramona lifted her glass and touched it lightly to each of ours before downing half of her drink in one gulp. "It's been a rough week."

"I'll say," I agreed. "I guess we all mourn in our own way."

"Ha!" She must have seen the shocked look on my face. "Ray and I have been separated about a hundred times. He always says he's going to turn over a new leaf. I don't know why, but I believe him every time. I guess a girl's gotta dream."

"But you were living together, weren't you?" I asked.

She downed the rest of her drink and looked around for the server. "I kicked him out of the house again a couple of days before he died. We'd got in a huge fight. This job with the recall committee was supposed to be on the up-and-up."

"And it wasn't?"

"It started out that way, or at least close enough." Ramona lowered her voice to just above a whisper. "I knew that Ray liked to bend the rules, and I figured that's why Jarman hired him to run the recall campaign. Turned out, his real job was to find dirt on the sheriff. He let Krissyanne do most of the grunt work when it came to the recall, like signing up people to distribute petitions or sending fundraising emails."

I hung on Ramona's every word. "And did he find dirt?"

She gave a rueful laugh. "Yeah, but not on Fontana. That old rumor about the two of you was about the only thing he could turn up. Turns out, our sheriff is clean as a whistle. But then, Ray tells me he has an idea. He could set him up."

"Set up Fontana? Like frame him?" Irma asked. "For what?"

"I don't think he'd figured that out yet." Ramona caught our server's eye and held up her empty glass. She swirled the ice cubes in the empty glass while waiting for her refill. "Ray said that he'd be getting a big payday if he pulled it off."

I sipped my wine, my mind whirling. "Do you think

Jarman might have decided to frame Fontana himself? And save himself the money?"

The server returned with Ramona's drink—her third at least.

"Yeah, that's sounds exactly like the sort of thing Jarman would do." Ramona took a big sip of the drink. "He loved to cut costs as much as he loved cutting corners. But murder?" She shook her head vigorously. "Nah. He would have framed Fontana for embezzlement or taking a bribe or something like that."

"What if he wanted to get rid of Ray and decided he could frame the sheriff at the same time?"

Ramona tossed her dark, wild hair over her shoulder. "Jarman doesn't get his hands dirty. That's why he hired Ray."

"Maybe he hired someone else?" I suggested.

"The whole reason Jarman came to me was because he doesn't know those sorts of people. It's not like you can just go on a website and find a hit man." She smirked. "At least, I don't advise it. I heard a story about a wife who hired someone to get rid of her husband. The guy went to the husband who paid him double."

The talk about contract killers made a chill run down my spine.

~

WHEN WE REALIZED RAMONA DIDN'T HAVE ANY OTHER valuable information, I paid the check and headed for the front door. A voice I recognized called my name, and it wasn't someone I wanted to run into. I turned and found myself face to face with Cheryl Fontana, the sheriff's wife.

I had no interest in talking with her. "I was just leaving."

"Not until I've had a word with you." Cheryl, dressed stylishly as always without a hair out of place, spoke in a pleasant tone, which didn't fool me for a minute.

"I'll wait for you by the car." Irma hurried out the door and I watched her leave, feeling abandoned.

"Fine." I looked Cheryl in the eye, doing my best to show I wasn't intimidated. "Say what you need to say."

"I gather you know that my husband and I are getting a divorce."

"I'm really not interested in any of the details of your personal life, or anything else concerning you, for that matter."

I turned to leave, but she grabbed my arm. Doing my best to shoot daggers at her with my eyes, I shook myself free.

She took a step closer and lowered her voice. "You can have him now. That's what you've been after all along, isn't it?" She said it as an accusation rather than a question.

I steadied my breathing, doing my best to keep my anger under control. "I'm not interested in married men. I never have been. But if you don't want him anymore, then I'm sure someone will snatch him up as quick as a Ferragamo purse off the sale rack." I figured she'd get the analogy. "Come to think of it, I'd better decide if I want to step in or I may lose my chance. Thanks for the suggestion."

"You little…"

I didn't wait to hear what name she'd call me. I was out the door and headed to the car before she could finish her sentence.

"You seem worked up," Irma said as I unlocked the car.

I didn't speak until we were on the road. "Great sidekick you are," I grumbled. "Leaving me to face my arch nemesis alone."

Irma grinned. "Ah heck, I knew you could handle her."

CHAPTER 19

J dropped off Irma at her house and headed home. I wanted nothing more than a nice cup of tea and about a gallon of chocolate cheesecake mousse. I hoped it would help me recover from my run-in with the sheriff's wife.

Jennifer's car was gone from the driveway, which meant I didn't have to share the mousse. The secret garden looked amazing from the outside with the new gate. My lawn, however, would need some time to recover from the heavy rain.

When I got settled in the kitchen, I changed my mind on my choice of beverage and poured myself a glass of white wine. I pulled the container of mousse out of the refrigerator and set it on the island, debating whether to dish out a reasonable portion or just dig in.

"You only live once." I retrieved a spoon and pulled off the lid.

Chef appeared, also holding a glass of wine, though his was red. "This is so true, *ma cherie.*"

I scooped up a spoonful of mousse just as Levi entered. I froze with the spoon halfway to my mouth, then set it down.

"I hope I'm not interrupting you." His voice had a hint of a drawl. Something about his voice made me melt—a velvety richness in his tone. I wouldn't mind listening to him read the phone book if I got the chance.

"What are you doing here so late?" I asked.

"I thought I could get started on the planting, or at least planning it out. I heard George say you'd like... how'd he put it... a mess of flowers and stuff, I think he said."

I chuckled. "That's not exactly how I phrased it, but I think you get the picture. I'd love plants that bloom at different times of the year so there are flowers most of the year, if that's possible."

"Considering the climate here, I don't see why not. What are your favorite flowers?"

"Roses, lavender..." My mind went blank, and I couldn't think of any other flowers at that moment. "I've got a lot going on right now. I'm sure whatever you pick will be great."

I glanced at Chef Emile, who raised his eyebrows.

"I can see I'm in your way," Levi said.

"No, no." Had I come across as rude? "I'm just preoccupied right now. I'm sure I'll be happy with whatever you choose." I remembered one thing I wanted. "I'd love fragrant flowers if possible."

Levi smiled. "Anything is possible in a magical place

like a secret garden. One more thing—what are your favorite colors?"

When was the last time I'd been asked that question? "I love purple. And blue. Pink, of course. Maybe a touch of yellow."

He nodded. "Sounds like your favorite color is all of them."

"Oh, I..."

He grinned, and the corners of his eyes crinkled. "That's my favorite color too." He said goodnight and slipped out the back door.

FIRST THING THE NEXT MORNING, I SENT A TEXT TO Irma and Freddie to meet me at my place. Freddie had patients to see, but said she'd stop by at lunch time.

"Are we opening today?" Jennifer asked as she handed me my morning cappuccino.

"Of course," I said. "Why wouldn't we?"

"We don't have a single reservation, and the weather report says ninety percent chance of rain."

"It does?" Living in a coastal town, I'd have to get better about checking the weather report. "When does the weather channel think the sun will show up again?"

"April."

"Yes?"

Jennifer blinked a few times in confusion. "No, I meant in April. The sun will come back in April. I was making a joke."

"A little one," I teased. I'd had plenty of jokes made

about my name over the years. They used to bother me, but I'd learned to make peace with having an interesting name.

While waiting for Irma, I made breakfast pizzas for Jennifer and me. Chef kept up a running commentary as I layered cheese, scrambled eggs and bacon on French bread.

"What is this abomination you are creating?" He stood close to me as he watched, making goosebumps run up and down my arm.

I popped the baking sheet in the oven then turned to give him a piece of my mind before I remembered Jennifer's presence. Instead, I made a face at him.

"Everything okay?" Jennifer asked. "You look like you're mad at someone. You're not mad at me, are you?"

"Of course not," I assured her.

I sat at the island with my back to the chef, but that didn't stop him from talking.

"I suppose you are angry with me," he complained. "Why? I am only trying to help."

I glanced over my shoulder, and Chef looked so sincere I felt bad for a moment. Then he kept talking and my sympathy evaporated.

"I have been doing my best to make a chef out of you, but I may have to accept that you simply do not have what it takes."

Irma arrived just as the timer buzzed. After removing the breakfast pizzas from the oven, I placed them on a serving plate for everyone to share.

"Where's Zoe?" I asked.

"Still asleep. We were up late talking. Making plans for the future. Nothing I'm ready to talk about yet—just bouncing around ideas."

"I'm glad you're not rushing into anything. Like moving to Istanbul." I suggested the three of us move to the front room. Jennifer and I carried our food and drinks to the sofa and chairs by the fireplace. I turned on the gas jets to take the chill out of the room. Everyone must have been enjoying the food because none of us spoke until we'd finished our last bites.

"Great breakfast." Irma set her plate down on the coffee table. "Why'd you want me to come over? Do we have another suspect to question?"

"I wish." I glanced at Jennifer, who took the hint that I wanted to speak with Irma alone.

She stood and collected our plates. "I'll clean up from breakfast and then I think I'll go upstairs. I've got some homework to catch up on."

As soon as Irma and I were alone, I spoke in hushed tones. "All of our suspects have rock-solid alibis. Ramona was at work. So was Jarman, her boss. Rugger has plenty of witnesses who saw him at sheriff's head-quarters. Yolanda—Deputy Lopez, that is—told me that she spoke to Rugger. Turns out, he showed up right after me because Quimby had asked for a meeting. Rugger claims he doesn't know what the meeting was going to be about."

"I never really thought he killed Quimby anyway," Irma said. "But it is disappointing that all of our suspects have alibis."

"All but the sheriff," I corrected. "Krissyanne was

picking up her friend's kid at the time of the murder. I feel like we're missing someone. Who else could have possibly killed Quimby?"

Irma thought for a moment. "A hit man? Maybe Ramona wanted her husband out of her life bad enough to hire someone."

"But what would her motive be?" I asked. "If she wanted to get rid of Quimby, she could just get a divorce."

"What about a life insurance policy? Do we know if Quimby had one?"

I shook my head. "I can ask Yolanda, but I still don't think Ramona hired a hit man. I don't believe it's as easy as you may think."

"Oh! I know." Irma bounced in her seat excitedly. "Jarman paid Ramona to kill her husband, promising he'd give her an alibi."

"There must be other people who saw both of them at work." I thought over what she'd said. "Although, with Ramona and Jarman being each other's alibis, it's worth checking into whether anyone else can corroborate their whereabouts at the time of the murder."

I called Deputy Lopez and left a message. She called me back minutes later.

"What have you got?" she asked hopefully.

"Sorry to disappoint you. I got nothing. I hoped you'd tell me that Ramona Quimby and Pierce Jarman have no one to verify their alibis but each other."

"Thinking they're in on it together, huh? Now it's my turn to disappoint. No less than ten coworkers confirmed they were all in a meeting at Superior Uniform Supply at the time of the murder."

"Then, maybe..." I hesitated to ask, hoping she wouldn't laugh at me. "They might have hired a hit man?"

"The details of the crime aren't consistent with a contract killing." She went on to explain how a hit man wouldn't want to be seen by his victim—it made it less personal. "Quimby's killer stood only ten feet or so away when they pulled the trigger."

"Are you saying he was probably shot by someone who knew him?"

"Someone who knew him and hated him, I would think," she said. "Or a cold-blooded killer."

A chill ran up my spine. "Maybe both."

~

IRMA GAVE ME A QUESTIONING LOOK AS I PUT MY PHONE down. Rain began to pelt the side of the house again, as if we hadn't had enough already.

"Ramona Quimby and Pierce Jarman have solid alibis." My shoulders slumped. "We're making no progress at all. Sheriff Fontana better make bail, or it looks like he's going to be behind bars for a long time."

The room darkened as black clouds gathered outside. The truth began to sink in, and an ugly thought formed. Every person we'd suspected of killing Ray Quimby had a rock-solid alibi—all but one. I got up and flicked on a nearby floor lamp.

"I hate to say it." I threw a log on the fire and sat

back on the sofa. "There's no one else who had the means, opportunity, and motive other than Sheriff Fontana."

Irma leaned forward in her chair. "What are you saying?"

I hated to say it out loud, but someone had to. "Maybe the sheriff is guilty. Maybe we let our feelings for him get in the way."

Irma stared at me, her expression a mix of frustration and disappointment. "April May, are you giving up?"

"Not giving up, exactly." I picked up one of the throw pillows and hugged it to my chest. "I think we need to face facts."

She jumped up, surprising me with her sudden energy. "I don't believe for a minute the sheriff is a killer."

"Calm down, Irma."

Her voice rose. "Calm down? You want me to calm down? I'll calm down when the person who killed Quimby is behind bars and not before." She grabbed her coat and headed for the front door.

"Wait!" I jumped up and chased after her, but before I reached the front door, she slammed it in my face. I stood by the window as she hustled to her car and drove off.

"Oh Irma." I stared at the street long after I lost sight of her car.

She'd be back when she cooled off.

CHAPTER 20

Freddie arrived in time for lunch, and I told her about Irma storming out. We sat in the kitchen eating bowls of stew and warm French bread while I sulked, unhappy that I had upset Irma. The rain had turned to a dreary drizzle, matching my mood.

Freddie dipped her buttered bread into the stew. "Irma has a loyal streak about a mile long. That's one of the things we love about her, but you witnessed the downside of that loyalty today. She'll cool off quick enough and then you can have a nice long talk."

"That's what I figured." Or at least hoped. "Can you think of someone else who might have killed Quimby? Someone other than the sheriff?" I wiped the last of the stew from my bowl with the bread and chewed slowly, forcing myself to think harder, as if that would help.

Freddie put our bowls in the dishwasher and returned to the island. "I can understand why Irma can't believe Fontana is a killer. I can't believe it either, but all the evidence points to him. I think we just have to face facts."

"That's what I told Irma." Some people didn't want to hear the truth. "Want some chocolate cheesecake mousse? I managed to keep from eating all of it."

After dessert, Freddie went back to her office. I checked my phone every five minutes or so to see if Irma had answered one of my twenty or so messages. By dinner time, I began to worry that she wouldn't get over it so quickly.

When the phone finally buzzed, it wasn't a text from Irma. It was Zoe.

Do you know where Irma is? Not answering my texts.

~

THIS WAS NO TIME FOR TEXTING—I HIT DIAL AND ZOE picked up on the first ring.

"I haven't seen her all day." Her voice shook with worry. "She sent me a text this morning, but now she's not texting me back. I tried about a hundred times."

"What did her last text say?" I asked.

"She was going to Somerton to investigate."

"Did she say what she was investigating? Or who she was seeing?"

"No. That's all it said."

I didn't want Zoe to be alone while we figured out if something had happened to Irma. "Hold on." I called up to Jennifer and she emerged at the top of the stairs. "Would you go pick up Zoe and bring her here?"

"Sure. Is something wrong?"

"I hope not." I really, really hoped not, but the sinking feeling in my stomach told me something was very wrong. I told Zoe that Jennifer was coming to get her and hung up.

Had Irma gone to question the wrong person? The idea that something bad might have happened to her made my blood run cold.

"No," I told myself as I grabbed my keys. "She's okay. She has to be okay."

The twenty-minute drive to Somerton felt like hours. On the way I called Deputy Lopez and shared my concerns with her. It was too soon to put out a missing person's report without any firm evidence that she was in danger, but Lopez said she'd see what she could do.

"This is why it's important to leave the investigating to the proper authorities," she said unnecessarily.

I hung up and headed straight for the recall headquarters.

KRISSYANNE SAT AT HER DESK, THE SAME DESK WHERE Quimby had once sat. She smiled brightly when I entered, quite different from the way she'd greeted me in the past.

"Hello again," she called out cheerfully. "It's April, right?"

"Yes, have you seen Irma Vargas?"

She tipped her head a few degrees to one side. "Who?"

"The older lady who came with me the other day. About so high?" I held my hand out shoulder height.

She pursed her lips and blinked a few times before giving her head a little shake. "I haven't seen her since then. Is something wrong?"

I forced a smile. "Probably not. But if you see her, would you tell her to call me? It's possible her phone just went dead, but I can't help but worry."

"I understand," she said sympathetically. "We do worry about our elders, don't we? Does she have memory issues?"

"What?" Her question took me aback. "No, not at all."

"I'm sorry, I just assumed. You'd think I'd have learned by now not to jump to conclusions. Did she say she was coming here again?"

"No, just that she was coming to Somerton to..." I stopped myself from saying "investigate." "To take care of some errands. I thought she might have come back to get the petitions she'd asked you about."

"When you see her, let her know that she can stop by and pick some up. I've gotten everything organized now."

"I will," I said absentmindedly and turned to go.

"I hope you find your friend," Krissyanne called out after me.

I stepped back onto the sidewalk with no idea where to go next.

"Where are you, Irma?"

∼

I SAT IN MY CAR IN FRONT OF THE RECALL headquarters, hopelessness threatening to drown me. Wiping my eyes on the sleeve of my shirt, I scolded myself. This was no time for tears—I needed a plan. I ticked off the suspects in my head one more time. What had I missed?

Who had I missed?

Sheriff Fontana was in jail, so he wasn't responsible for Irma's disappearance... unless he had an accomplice. But who would that even be? Cheryl? I dismissed that idea immediately. I'd be surprised if Fontana and his wife were even talking to each other.

What about Rugger? Was the talk about Fontana and Rugger's feud a smokescreen to cover up their joint involvement in some scheme? Had Irma gone to question him and gotten too close to the truth? I called Deputy Lopez again and asked her if she could check if Irma had been to Rugger's office.

Then I remembered that Rugger had put the sheriff in jail. I doubted that they'd go that far to make it appear that they were enemies. Still, I wasn't ready to rule it out.

I could drive over to the sheriff's headquarters and ask to speak to Rugger, but first, I'd swing by Superior Uniform and see if Ramona would talk to me. Maybe she knew something she hadn't thought to mention—something that seemed unimportant to her but that might be an important clue.

A few blocks away I changed my mind and pulled into the grocery store parking lot. If Irma was in danger, every minute might count, and traipsing around Somerton without a real plan seemed like a waste of time. I needed to be more efficient.

A trapped feeling came over me as I fought back panic. *Think, April. Think.* First, I would call Ramona instead of seeing her in person, then I'd decide what to do next. Hoping some fresh air would help me focus, I got out of the car and pulled up Ramona's number.

A weary looking mother passed me pushing a shopping cart and holding the hand of a little girl who skipped alongside her. The child looked familiar. They'd nearly reached their car before I placed her as the girl Krissyanne had been babysitting the night of the murder.

"Hi," I said to the mother, who gave me a suspicious look. I forced myself to smile, hoping I looked friendly despite my internal agitation. "You're Krissyanne's friend, aren't you?"

She glared at me. "Some friend." Her little girl stared at me with wide eyes.

"Oh, is this about the… incident at the recall headquarters?" I chose my words carefully, remembering my mother's phrase—*little pitchers have big ears.*

She put one hand on her hip. "You know about that? Well, did you know that she wasn't even supposed to pick my kid up that day? I show up to her school and find out that Krissyanne decided to take her out for ice cream. Except they went straight to the recall office where you-know-who was you-know-what."

"Do you know what time she picked her up?" When she hesitated, I urged, "It might be important."

Confusion replaced her anger. "Really?" She

thought for a moment. "The teacher said I missed her by five or ten minutes, and I got there right around five. What's this about?"

"Thanks." I hurried to my car before she could ask more questions. Everything came into focus, and I felt certain where to find Irma. What I'd just been told meant Krissyanne had no alibi, and that could only mean one thing.

Krissyanne was the murderer.

CHAPTER 21

$\mathcal{I}$ drove the half-mile back to the recall headquarters as fast as I could without risking an accident. On the way, I left messages for Molina and Lopez, annoyed that neither of them answered their phones when I most needed them. A voice in the back of my brain told me to wait for one of them to call me back, but if I delayed, it might be too late, and I might never see Irma again. I pushed the thought from my mind.

Screeching to a halt in front of the recall headquarters, half in the red zone, I jumped out of the car and shoved on the front door, but it didn't budge. Instead, my body slammed against the glass.

"Ow." That hurt.

Stepping back, I stared at the sign in the window. Closed.

I squinted into the dim interior and movement caught my eye. "Hey."

Krissyanne sat behind the desk, calmly staring at

the screen. I banged on the door to get her attention. She turned her head in my direction, her face expressionless.

"Let me in," I mouthed, not sure if she could hear me. When she didn't move, I banged on the door again and called out more loudly. "Let me in. Now."

My heart pounded against my ribcage as I watched her slowly rise and head toward me. She stood on the other side of the door as if deciding whether to open it or not. After a long moment, she turned the lock and stepped back from the door.

Holding my breath, I pushed the door open.

I willed my voice to be steady. "Hello again, Krissyanne." Irma's life might depend on my acting skills and quick thinking.

"What are you doing back again so soon?" Krissyanne's voice sounded flat.

"I just remembered I'd dropped something the night Quimby was killed. You don't mind if I take a quick look, do you?" Without waiting for an answer, I headed for the back of the large room where there must be a storeroom of some kind. If Krissyanne had Irma locked away somewhere, this might be the place.

"I do mind, actually." Krissyanne grabbed my arm to stop me.

I turned to face her. "Oh, okay." I smiled, hoping it didn't look like a grimace. "Hiding something?"

"Not at all," she said. "But there are proprietary and confidential files stored back there."

I shrugged and forced a casual attitude as I pried

her hand from my arm. "Oh, well. I guess it's not that important."

We stood staring at each other for several seconds, as if waiting to see who would make the first move. It would have helped to have a plan, but it was too late now. I'd have to take my chances and hope for the best.

I spun on my heel and ran toward the back of the offices. To the right of the exit was another door, as I'd guessed. I grabbed the doorknob and twisted it, but it didn't budge. In a panic, I banged on the door, then held my ear against it, straining to hear inside.

Was that a thump?

"Irma? Is that you?"

A noise behind me made me turn around just in time to duck and avoid a heavy glass vase aimed at my head. It crashed against the wall and splintered into hundreds of pieces.

"Irma's in there, isn't she?" My mind told me to run and get help, but surrounded by pieces of the broken vase, running was out of the question. One slip and I'd be a pincushion full of glass shards.

Krissyanne must have realized my predicament, since she leisurely returned to her desk. The moment she turned her back on me, I picked up the biggest piece of broken glass I could see and held it gingerly in my hand.

With a weapon in hand, a shot of adrenaline coursed through me and my confidence grew. That confidence deflated when I saw what Krissyanne had gone back to get from her desk.

A gun was pointed straight at my chest.

CHAPTER 22

I nearly dropped my glass weapon. What good would it do against a gun?

"Why, Krissyanne?" My voice sounded feeble in my ears.

"Why what?" She thrust her shoulders back in defiance. "Why did I kill Ray?"

"So, you admit it." Not that her confession was going to do me any good. I had no doubt I'd soon be locked in the storeroom with Irma. That was if Krissyanne didn't shoot me.

She huffed. "I didn't do it on purpose, but when he found out about the money, he threatened to go to Mr. Jarman and get me fired or even arrested. I told him go ahead—I'd tell our boss all about all the money Ray had taken."

"You *both* embezzled from the campaign?"

She gave an indignant flip of her hair. "If he was going to get rich siphoning off donations, why shouldn't I?"

I assumed it was a rhetorical question. "Okay. He caught you with your hands in the cookie jar, so you accused him of stealing. Seems to me the two of you could have formed a profitable partnership. What happened?"

"He laughed at me." Krissyanne's face contorted in anguish, as if being laughed at was the worst thing that could happen to someone. "Then he called me an amateur. An amateur!"

Apparently, being called an amateur was even worse than being laughed at.

I had so many questions, but I blurted out, "So you shot him? For laughing at you?"

She pouted. "I just wanted to wipe that annoying grin off his face, so I got the gun out of my desk and pointed it right at his chest."

"What did he do?" I wanted to learn the whole story, but more importantly I hoped to stall her. Eventually someone had to show up to save the day—hopefully one of the sheriff's deputies or, even better, the whole department.

"He laughed again." Her voice expressed disbelief.

"He didn't." I wouldn't have laughed at someone pointing a gun at me. I certainly wasn't laughing at Krissyanne, whose grip appeared firm on the pistol aimed at my heart. "You'd think he would have had better sense. Of course, I didn't know the guy, but he sure did seem full of himself at the press conference in his fancy, royal-blue suit."

"You have no idea."

She seemed to relax, and the aim of the gun lowered

an inch or two, giving me hope. It was now pointed at my stomach, and I considered the odds of surviving a bullet wound to the belly. It had to be better than a chest wound.

She smiled, something between a sneer and an evil grin. "I'm almost starting to like you." My hopes evaporated when she added, "Too bad I have to kill you."

"But do you?" I spoke in my best "I'm on your side" voice, soothing and understanding. "Just lock me in the storeroom with Irma and skip town. By the time we manage to get out, you could be in Bermuda." Or wherever murderous thieves went these days. "I mean, do you really want to have to dispose of a body? It's harder than you might think. Just last year, someone threw their husband off a boat, and he washed up on shore just a few days later."

Krissyanne chewed on one corner of her lower lip while she considered this. "You know, I think you're right. I've been working to cover up my tracks and make it look like Ray took all the money." She sighed longingly. "I really wanted to take over his job. I would have been so good at it. But maybe it's time for a change of plans."

I felt my shoulders relax. She wasn't going to kill me after all. Irma and I might get out of this alive, and if we did, we were going to have a long talk about putting ourselves in dangerous situations.

Krissyanne reached behind her and shuffled around in the desk drawer, finally retrieving a roll of duct tape. "I'll put you in the storeroom for now. With no food or water, you'll be dead in a few days. And by the time your bodies are found, I'll be long gone."

Her words stole the hope from my soul, but I hoped if I kept her talking, help would arrive in time to save Irma and me.

"How'd you manage to plant the laptop and gun at Sheriff Fontana's home?" I asked.

Her eyes lit up with pride. "That was even easier than I thought it would be. You'd think the sheriff would have a first-class security system, wouldn't you?" She chuckled at the memory. "No alarm, no deadbolt, nothing. I managed to pick the lock on the back door in about five minutes."

Keeping her eyes on me and the gun pointed once again at my chest, Krissyanne opened another drawer and grabbed a length of rope.

Was this it? After everything I'd done my entire life, all the accomplishments and failures, brilliant decisions and stupid mistakes, is this where it would all end? As far as stupid mistakes went, coming to rescue Irma all by myself might have been the biggest I'd ever made. Why didn't I wait for backup?

I thought of Irma tied up and trapped in the storeroom behind me. Scared and all alone. I heard her voice in my mind: "Are you giving up?"

"Hold your hands out in front of you," Krissyanne instructed, and I complied.

When she held out the rope, I took a chance. I jabbed the broken shard of glass into her wrist. She cried out in pain and the gun went off. I felt a sharp pain in my thigh as the gun fell to the ground with a clunk.

"You witch." Krissyanne clutched her arm, and I jabbed again as she lunged for the gun. She lost her balance and fell on her hands and knees onto the broken glass. As she shrieked in pain, I carefully slid across the floor like an ice skater, keeping my feet flat on the ground to avoid slipping and joining her on the floor. I picked up the gun but didn't bother pointing it at her.

Krissyanne lay on the ground, moaning and covered in blood from the injury I'd inflicted as well as hundreds of tiny other cuts. She wasn't a threat to me at the moment, but I wasn't taking any chances. I watched her carefully, ready to shoot her if she made a wrong move.

As I pulled out my phone, the front door opened. Deputy Rugger pulled his gun when he saw us.

"Drop the gun," he shouted.

I tossed the gun aside and turned to face him, my arms held up. "There's your murderer," I said, pointing at Krissyanne's pathetic figure, moaning and covered in blood. "And Irma Vargas is locked up in the storeroom. I need to let her out. *Now.*" I emphasized the last word, not wanting Irma to be trapped for one more moment than necessary.

"Don't move," Rugger ordered, his gun trained on me.

Barely able to keep my voice steady, I quickly explained that Krissyanne had murdered Quimby and planned to leave the country with money she'd embezzled from the recall committee. As Rugger's gaze moved from me to Krissyanne, I told him about the little girl she'd used as an alibi.

"She picked up her friend's kid after the murder." I did my best to keep my voice calm. "The girl's mother will confirm the time. Then Krissyanne came right back here and pretended to be shocked that Quimby had been shot."

Krissyanne seemed to have found her voice. She held up a bloody hand and waved it at Rugger. "That's not true," she whined. "She's the one who killed Quimby."

Rugger didn't seem to know who to believe.

"Just open the storeroom door and let my friend out," I said. "Please."

"No." Krissyanne whimpered and began to cry. "They're trying to frame me."

"Who is?" Rugger asked.

"She is." Krissyanne pointed at me accusingly. "And her nosy old friend."

"Her friend?" Rugger took a step closer, then became aware of the broken glass all over the floor and stopped. "Did you lock someone in the storeroom, Krissyanne?"

Krissyanne's eyes widened and she shut her mouth tightly.

I felt a glimmer of hope. "Where are the keys to the storeroom?" When she turned away defiantly, I said to Rugger, "Try her desk drawer or maybe her purse."

After several minutes while I waited anxiously, Rugger found the keys and handed them to me. Being careful to avoid slipping on the broken glass, I made my way to the storeroom and unlocked the door. Flicking on the light, I cried out in relief. In a corner, her wrists and ankles bound with rope and her mouth taped, Irma blinked in the harsh light. I hurried over to hug her.

While I struggled to loosen the knots, Irma tried to speak. I yanked off the duct tape and she yelped.

"Sorry!"

"Sorry for what?" she grumbled. "For taking so dang long to come rescue me?" She couldn't hide her relief, and I hugged her again.

I finally let go of her and went back to work on the knots. "Well, you see, I had a nail appointment and some shopping to do, so…" My words stuck in my throat and the reality that I might have lost Irma forever began to sink in. I struggled to catch my breath.

"What's wrong? Are you hyperventilating? Do you need a paper bag?" Her sarcastic tone reassured me somehow and kept me from turning into a blithering blob.

I laughed. "You're the one who was kidnapped."

Her voice became serious. "But you're bleeding. You've been shot!"

"Nah, that's just Krissyanne's blood." I stood and felt a sharp pain in my thigh. Reaching for my leg, it felt wet. I stared at my hand. "That's a lot of blood."

The room began to spin.

CHAPTER 23

"You took a bullet?" Jennifer sounded more impressed than worried as she wheeled me to the elevator. "I've never taken a bullet."

"Let's keep it that way, okay?"

The hospital insisted that Irma and I leave in wheelchairs, and Freddie got the job of wheeling Irma, who complained nonstop.

"I'm perfectly capable of walking," Irma insisted. "I don't know why everyone's treating me like an invalid. I didn't even get shot."

The bullet had only grazed my thigh, and I had some superficial cuts on my hand from the broken glass when I grabbed the gun from the floor, but other than that, I'd never felt better. The doctor wanted to keep Irma overnight for observation due to dehydration, but she refused.

"You can't keep me here against my will," Irma had informed them.

I caught the doctor rolling his eyes. He turned to Freddie. "Maybe you can reason with her."

Freddie chuckled. "That would be a first." She reassured the doctor that she'd keep an eye on both of us.

On the drive back to Serenity Cove, I took the back seat, hoping to have a few quiet moments. Irma and I would soon enough be peppered with questions.

Irma couldn't wait to tell us about her run-in with Krissyanne, and I leaned forward to hear her tell Freddie how she'd ended up in the storeroom.

"I figured Krissyanne must have known more than what she was letting on, but it never occurred to me that she'd killed Quimby. I thought she had an airtight alibi. That's what April told me."

"Yeah, about that…" I began. "Turns out, after she shot Quimby, she realized she'd be the first one they'd suspect. So, she went to the school and picked up her friend's daughter from her after-school program. Then she came right back to the office, where she planned to discover the body and call paramedics. When she found me and Rugger there, it made it even better."

"Why is that?" Freddie asked.

"Because she had witnesses and an audience. Her performance had me completely fooled and I'm pretty sure Rugger bought it hook, line, and sinker. You should have seen her. Krissyanne went through all the emotions—first shock, then disbelief, then wailing with grief."

Irma huffed. "All the while, an innocent child looking on. Poor thing."

"Luckily, she didn't see the body." I still thought it

was an awful thing to show up to a crime scene with a young girl in hand. I tapped Irma on the shoulder. "Finish your story. You went to question Krissyanne?"

"Dumb idea. I know. You don't have to rub it in."

I shrugged. "Not so dumb. I went to rescue you alone, remember?"

Irma's expression brightened. "How could I forget? Anyway, I must have asked one too many questions. She seemed edgy somehow, so I just kept digging. I figured I was onto something when she pulled the gun out of her desk drawer."

"You must have been terrified," Freddie said.

"I was too stunned to be terrified, I think. I hoped if I just did what she told me that I'd get out alive. She hog-tied me and taped my mouth shut."

"That must have been the hardest part," I quipped.

Irma reached behind her and smacked my knee. "You're on my good side since you came to rescue me, but it's a short trip to get on my bad side. Don't push your luck."

I laughed, happy that Irma sounded like her old self. Leaning back in my seat, a warm feeling of contentment washed over me.

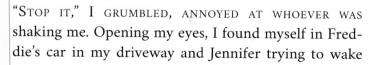

"STOP IT," I GRUMBLED, ANNOYED AT WHOEVER WAS shaking me. Opening my eyes, I found myself in Freddie's car in my driveway and Jennifer trying to wake me up. Worry showed in her eyes. Behind her in the middle of the front yard, Levi stood watching us. I smiled and gave him a little wave.

Jennifer leaned over me. "Oh, good. You're awake." Zoe stood next to her, and I marveled at how young people can become fast friends in a matter of days.

"How's the secret garden coming?" I called out to Levi, but he'd gone.

"Is that all you can think about?" Jennifer asked. "It's nearly done, believe it or not." She reached out a hand to help me out of the car, but I brushed her off.

"And George didn't have a stroke or anything?" Irma asked.

"Good thing he had Levi to help." I climbed out of the car and slammed the door.

"Who's Levi?" Irma took Zoe's arm and they headed for the porch steps. "Are you holding out on me?"

"It's straight to the sofa for both of you," Freddie ordered. "I want you to rest for the rest of the day and all day tomorrow."

I nudged Jennifer's arm. "Good thing I have you to wait on me hand and foot."

Jennifer grinned. "Me and Zoe. We'll take care of you two."

True to their word, Jennifer and Zoe pampered us for the rest of the day, even preparing us dinner. Luckily, I had a freezer full of soup that was easily reheated. Add a few slices of French bread, and we had a delicious meal. Freddie returned in the evening to take Irma and Zoe home.

"Rest up," she ordered me. "I'll take you and Irma to pick up your cars tomorrow."

I vaguely remembered parking in the red zone. "Hopefully they didn't tow mine."

Jennifer sent me to bed early. As I lay in bed, my mind raced, but exhaustion got the better of me and I soon drifted off. I dreamt of running barefoot through glass shards and woke up with the bright sun streaming through my window. The events of the previous day came flooding back to me, and I counted my blessings. Surviving to see another day was at the top of my list.

Being alive was a wonderful thing.

CHAPTER 24

Freddie refused to let me work on Friday, so we stayed closed one more day. The phone kept ringing, and Jennifer reported regularly on our weekend reservations. By the time we opened on Saturday, we had a line waiting outside and we stayed busy the entire day.

Jennifer entered the kitchen and picked up a tea tray I'd just filled with sandwiches, quiches, flaky pastries, and mini eclairs. "I think everyone just wants to hear about your adventures."

I chuckled, not at all surprised. "I never thought the key to a successful tearoom would be a steady supply of gossip."

Jennifer paused before stepping into the front room. "In the future, do you think the gossip could involve something other than murder?"

Sunday turned out to be even busier, with a steady flow of diners from opening until closing. By Sunday afternoon, my feet ached, and I fantasized about curling up with a good book for at least a week.

When the last customer had left, I plopped on a stool at the island. I laid my head on the crook of my arm, barely looking up as Jennifer carried the last of the dishes in from the tearoom.

"I can finish up here," she said. "You rest up. There's not that much more to do."

I lifted my head. "Why aren't you tired? Oh, I forgot. You're young." Under my breath I added, "And I'm old."

She laughed. "You're not old, April. In fact, you're one of the most young-at-heart people I know. I suppose confronting a murderer and getting shot at must be tiring."

"You have no idea." I laid my head back down. "I think I'll stick to baking and serving tea from now on."

Jennifer finished the dishes and went upstairs. Chef hadn't been in the kitchen all day, and I felt a pang of worry before I remembered what he'd told me. "I am always here."

As tired as I was, I wanted to get a look at the progress George had made on my secret garden. When I stepped out the back door, I spotted Levi standing in front of the stone walls holding the gate open for me.

I made my way along the path to the garden entrance. Trembling with excitement, I reminded myself Levi and George couldn't have planted much yet. Still, that would be the easy part, or at least easier than building a six-foot stone wall.

"You have some visitors." Levi beckoned me to enter.

I stepped into the garden and gasped. Climbing vines covered in blue and purple blossoms climbed the outer wall. Stepping stones led past rose bushes and flowering shrubs to a swing hung from a branch of the old elm tree. A couple lazily swung back and forth, the man's arm around the woman's shoulder.

Without his chef's hat and shirt, it took me a moment to recognize Emile.

"Emile!" I cried out as if I hadn't seen him in years.

Chef's face beamed, his eyes sparkling with joy. "Mademoiselle, I would like to present to you—"

"Marie!" I hurried over to the petite woman with huge brown eyes and long, golden hair. "I can't tell you how happy I am to finally meet you."

Marie blinked and turned to Chef who gave her a reassuring nod.

He took her hand, squeezing it gently. "I have told Miss May all about you. It is she who convinced me to ask heaven to send you back to me."

She smiled, a sweet, radiant expression that I felt in my soul. "I am only here for a little while."

Chef's face fell. *"Zut alors.* You would not leave me so soon now that we are at last reunited."

"Mais non," Marie said softly. "I will never leave you again. You shall come with me."

I hesitated, not wanting to intrude on their conversation, but aware that it might be the last time I saw Chef Emile Toussaint. After one last look at the two lovebirds, I crept away and followed the path back to the garden entrance.

Levi waited for me by the open gate.

"You can see ghosts too?" I asked.

He cocked his head to one side. "Well of course."

The truth hit me like a ton of bricks. "Right." I forced a smile. "Because you're a ghost too."

CHAPTER 25

Spring arrived, along with warmer temperatures and more reservations for afternoon tea. The kitchen seemed empty without Chef. I hadn't realized how accustomed I'd become to his presence.

I reached for one of his cookbooks and stared at the picture on the back. I wiped away a tear as Jennifer pushed open the door carrying a stack of teacups.

"Everything okay?" she asked.

I nodded. I could hardly explain to her about missing a ghost when she didn't know about Chef.

"Maybe you should talk to yourself." She carefully set the teacups and saucers next to the sink. "That always seems to cheer you up. Or…" She snickered. "You could have an argument like you used to do."

"Yeah, about that." I leaned against the counter. "You may not believe this, but when I first moved into this house, I saw a ghost." I waited for her reaction, but she merely raised an eyebrow.

"And?"

"Is that all you have to say? I just told you I can see ghosts."

She brushed my confession away with a wave of her arm. "I know all about Chef Emile Toussaint."

"You do?" My mouth dropped open in disbelief.

"Sure. My grandma told me how he's been trapped in your kitchen ever since he tried to help her escape her abusive husband. She said he's a hero."

"Why didn't you say anything all these months?" I remembered all the times I'd pretended I'd been talking to myself when she caught me in the middle of a conversation with my ghost chef.

"Why didn't you ever tell me about him?"

That was a good question, and it took me a few moments to answer. "I was afraid you'd think I was crazy. I didn't want you to change your opinion of me or be uncomfortable around me."

"Because you can see ghosts?" Jennifer tilted her head to one side. "You're a good person, April. And you're good to me. That's all I care about." She paused and narrowed her eyes. "You're not a witch, are you?"

I laughed. "No, definitely not a witch."

"Darn. I guess you'll have to wash those teacups the old-fashioned way then. I'd better get back to our guests."

Alone again, I sighed. "I suppose I should be happy to have a ghost-free kitchen. I can cook and bake however I want without anyone scolding me."

Jennifer pushed the door open a sliver. "Is he back?"

"No. He's not coming back. I'll tell you all about it

after we close for the day. It's a lovely story, really. A happy ending."

"I like happy endings." Jennifer slipped back into the tearoom, leaving me alone in the kitchen.

A shiver ran up my spine. Was I alone?

My voice barely more than a whisper, I called out, "Who's there?"

The wall clocked ticked the seconds as I waited for a response. A transparent stranger appeared next to the stove. I squinted at his hazy image, like a video out of focus. I guessed him to be in his thirties when he died, which must have been a least a hundred years earlier based on his clothing. He wore a three-piece suit and top hat.

"Who are you?" I asked.

"Finally." He sighed with relief and tipped his hat. "My name is Zebediah Wooledge."

"Nice to meet you, Zebediah. Perhaps I should rephrase my question. What are you doing in my kitchen?"

"Are you April May?"

"I am," I admitted, still waiting for him to answer my question. My curiosity prompted another. "When did you die?" When my question was met with raised eyebrows, I added, "You do know you're dead, right?"

He nodded his head sadly. "I do. I've been dead for three days now. It's been quite an adjustment, as you might imagine."

"Three days?" I gestured at his apparel. "Are you sure?"

He tilted his head to one side. "It feels like a really

long time, but I'm a newbie at this whole ghost thing. Probably why it took me so long to get your attention."

"But why are you dressed like that?"

He chuckled. "Well, the last thing I did was appear in the role of Jack Worthing to a sold-out performance of *The Importance of Being Ernest*. I suppose I'm destined to wear these clothes for eternity."

"I suppose so." I didn't know the rules for ghosts.

He smiled pleasantly as if he had all the time in the world, which I supposed he did. I grew impatient, wanting to know if I'd gained a new kitchen ghost.

"So, what can I do for you?" I would normally offer a visitor a cup of tea, but Zebediah wouldn't be able to enjoy it.

The ghost took a step closer, his expression serious. "Find out who murdered me."

~

Book 7 in the Haunted Tearoom Cozy Mystery series is coming in Spring 2023!

Tea is for Temptation

Sign up for my (mostly) weekly email with updates, sales, freebies, and other fun stuff!
(Not to mention stories about my rescue dog Kit

including pictures).
https://karensuewalker.com

And read on for recipes!

RECIPES

VEGAN BLUEBERRY PANCAKES

Yield: 6-8 pancakes

INGREDIENTS:

- 1 cup all-purpose flour
- 2 Tablespoon granulated sugar
- 1 Tablespoon (not teaspoon!) baking powder
- ½ teaspoon salt
- 1 cup unsweetened soy milk, almond milk or other non-dairy milk
- 1 teaspoon vanilla extract
- 1 cup fresh or frozen blueberries
- Oil for the skillet or griddle if needed
- Maple syrup, jam, or other toppings

INSTRUCTIONS:

1. In a medium bowl, mix dry ingredients--
   flour, baking powder, baking soda, and salt.
2. Add almond or other non-dairy milk and
   vanilla and mix just until blended—don't
   overmix. Fold in blueberries.
3. Allow batter to rest for 5-10 minutes while
   you preheat skillet or griddle over medium
   low to medium heat. Wipe a small amount of
   oil (a teaspoon or so) on the skillet surface.
   Test heat by sprinkling a few water droplets
   on the surface. When they skitter and dance,
   the skillet is ready.
4. Scoop batter by ¼ cup measure onto the
   skillet. Cook for 2-3 minutes until the
   pancake is covered in small, popped bubbles.
   Flip and cook other side for about 2 minutes
   or until golden brown. If the pancakes are
   thicker than you prefer, you can add a little
   more non-dairy milk.
5. Serve pancakes or transfer to baking sheet
   and place in a 200F oven to keep warm.
6. Repeat process with remaining batter adding
   more oil to the skillet if needed. Serve
   immediately with maple syrup, jam, or other
   accompaniments.

April's note: You can freeze leftovers (if there are any!)
and heat them up in your toaster oven.

～

MADELEINES

Note: This recipe is adapted one developed by Sam at sugarspunrun.com. Check out all her great recipes!

Yield: 24 cookies

INGREDIENTS:

For coating the pan:

- 1 Tablespoon unsalted butter
- 1 ½ teaspoons all-purpose flour

For madeleines:

- 10 Tablespoons unsalted butter
- 2 large eggs
- ½ cup granulated sugar
- 3 Tablespoons light brown sugar, firmly packed
- 2 teaspoons vanilla extract
- 1/8 teaspoon salt
- 1 ¼ cup all-purpose flour

INSTRUCTIONS:

1. Preheat the oven to 375F (190C). Grease and flour 24 molds in your madeleine pan.
2. Melt 10 Tablespoons butter and set aside to cool.
3. In a large bowl, whisk eggs, white and brown sugar, vanilla, and salt until thoroughly combined.
4. Sift flour into the egg mixture, gently stirring to mix.
5. Drizzle cooled melted butter around the edge of the batter and fold in until thoroughly combined but not overmixed.
6. Spoon batter into 24 molds of your prepared pan—they should be about ¾ full.
7. Optional: Chill unbaked madeleines for ½ to 1 hour to make them rise more.
8. Bake in preheated oven at 375F (190C) for 9 minutes or until madeleines are light golden brown and spring back when lightly touched. (If your oven bakes unevenly, turn the pan around in the middle of baking.) Transfer cookies to a cooling rack.
9. If desired, sprinkle madeleines with powdered sugar or dip in melted chocolate before serving.

April's note: In case they aren't gobbled up immediately, they will keep in an airtight container at room temperature for a few days.

~

HOMEMADE MARSHMALLOWS

Yield: 30-40 large marshmallows

INGREDIENTS:

- Neutral flavored vegetable oil or shortening for greasing dish
- 1 cup powdered sugar (125g)
- ½ cup cornstarch (65g)
- ½ cup cold water
- 3 packets gelatin
- 2 cups granulated sugar
- 1 cup light corn syrup
- ½ cup water
- ¼ teaspoon salt
- 1 Tablespoon vanilla extract or vanilla bean paste

INSTRUCTIONS:

1. Thoroughly grease a 13" x 9" pan (or smaller for fatter marshmallows) with vegetable oil

or shortening. Also, grease rubber spatula and set aside for later.

2. Whisk together powdered sugar and cornstarch and set aside.

3. Combine the three packets of gelatin with ½ cup cold water in the bowl of a stand mixer fitted with whisk attachment. Set aside.

4. In a medium saucepan, combine sugar, corn syrup, ½ cup cold water, and salt. Stir to combine.

5. Cook at medium to medium-high heat stirring occasionally until mixture comes to a boil.

6. Attach candy thermometer and cook without stirring until mixture reaches 240F (115C) which should take about 10 minutes. (Make sure thermometer doesn't hit the bottom of the pan).

7. Turn mixer on low and carefully drizzle syrup into the gelatin mixture. Once all the syrup is added, increase mixer speed to medium then high.

8. Beat on high speed for 10 minutes (or longer if needed) until it is thick and stiff and greatly increased in volume.

9. Stir in vanilla until combined.

10. Spread marshmallow mixture into prepared pan and smooth the surface with your greased spatula.

11. Let marshmallows sit until firm at room temperature 4-6 hours or overnight or 2 hours in the refrigerator.

12. Sift a generous amount of the powdered sugar/cornstarch mixture onto a cutting board or other working surface and turn out the marshmallows onto it--it should come out in one sticky piece.

13. Use a sharp, greased knife or kitchen shears to cut into squares (clean and dry the knife or shears when they get sticky).

14. Toss marshmallows in remaining sugar/cornstarch mix and store in an airtight container at room temperature for up to 4 days.

April's note 1: You can use a high-powered hand mixer, but your results may vary (and your arm may get tired). You can also substitute additional powdered sugar for the cornstarch, but your marshmallows will be sweeter. (Maybe you think that's not a bad thing!)

April's note 2: You can add peppermint extract, other flavoring, or food color when you add the vanilla.

QUICK AND EASY SUGAR-FREE CHOCOLATE CHEESECAKE MOUSSE

Yield: 2 servings

INGREDIENTS:

- 4 ounces regular or light (NOT whipped) cream cheese, softened
- ½ cup heavy cream
- 1 teaspoon vanilla extract
- 2-3 Tablespoons Zero-calorie powdered sweetener
- 2 Tablespoons cocoa powder

INSTRUCTIONS:

1. Using an electric mixer, beat cream cheese until fluffy. On low speed, add in heavy cream and vanilla.
2. Add sweetener and cocoa and mix until well blended, then beat on high until light and fluffy—about 1-2 minutes.
3. Serve right away or refrigerate to serve later.
4. Garnish with unsweetened whipped cream or whipped topping, graham crackers, strawberries, coconut, or other toppings if desired.

April's note: For those who don't mind sugar, you can replace the sweetener with 2 Tablespoons powdered sugar. Yum!

What's next for April May?

TEA IS FOR TEMPTATION

A Haunted Tearoom Cozy Mystery #7 - Coming in Spring 2023

There's a new ghost in town, and he wants April to solve his murder. Is this April's new destiny—to be a ghost detective? Find out in Tea is for Temptation.

For all of Karen Sue Walker's books, visit https://karensuewalker.com/books

- *Haunted Tearoom Cozy Mysteries*
- *Bridal Shop Cozy Mysteries*
- *Arrow Investigations Humorous Action-Adventure Mysteries by KC Walker*

Visit https://karensuewalker/kcwalker to download **The Black Daiquiri**, a free novella featuring unemployed stuntwoman Whit Leland, her grandmother, and their rogue Chihuahua. Only available on my website!

Old Fashioned Murder, by KC Walker

Arrow Investigations Action-Adventure Mystery Book 1

Whitley "Whit" Leland is an out-of-work stuntwoman with an attitude. Stuck in a sleepy mountain village with her wannabe PI grandmother, Bobbie, she's content to spend her time eating flaky pastries, mixing cocktails, and chasing after her wayward rescue dog.

She also needs to keep her grandmother out of trouble, which is harder than she expects. Between rehearsals with the Ukulele Ladies, Bobbie investigates a series of seemingly unrelated accidents targeting local musicians. Whit enjoys teasing Bobbie about her true crime obsession--after all, who would go to such lengths just to win a small-town music competition?

Whit gets her answer when she finds one of the Ukulele Ladies dead. Is Bobbie next on the hit list? Whit will have to use her smarts and her skills to track down the murderer before they know she's onto them.

Can Whit, her grandmother, and their rogue chihuahua find the murderer before someone else turns up dead?

Available on Amazon now!

Made in United States
North Haven, CT
17 December 2022

29141623R00124